A Christmas Conspiracy

A Faith-Based Fiction Thriller, Volume 2

Jimmy Gear

Published by Jimmy Gear, 2024.

This is a work of fiction. Similarities to real people, places, or events are entirely coincidental.

A CHRISTMAS CONSPIRACY

First edition. November 15, 2024.

ISBN: 979-8227107800

Written by Jimmy Gear.

Also by Jimmy Gear

A Faith-Based Fiction Thriller
Captive Memory
A Christmas Conspiracy

For the good folks at Pleasant Valley Baptist Church,
who've only given me the most merry of Christmases!

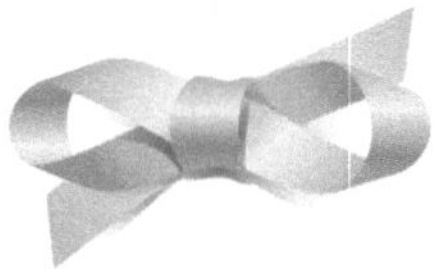

A CHRISTMAS CONSPIRACY
BY: JIMMY GEAR

DECEMBER 22nd

ONE

Aria Chambers was looking forward to a quiet, uneventful Christmas. Without family nearby and several days off coming up, she was excited about curling up on the couch with a good Christmas movie and some hot chocolate.

She lived in a rural town of about ten thousand people in the middle of Nebraska. Not as small a town as some, but not nearly as large or remarkable as others. But that's exactly what Aria Chambers liked about Anderson's Crossroads: There were the usual fast-food chains, clothing stores and other amenities, but there was also a general feeling of civic pride and safety. The last place that one would guess that danger would come calling.

In ignorance of the approaching danger, the entire town had succumbed to the festive trappings of late December: Yards were overrun by blow-up mascots of the season—Here was Frosty, there a Rudolph, over in another yard the Grinch was stealthily sneaking toward the front door; Candy cane posts flanked freshly paved sidewalks; and many a front door was decked with colorful garlands and wreaths. The city council had even organized the decoration of every light pole in the square, the motto "'Tis the Season" emblazoned in gold upon a backdrop of red. Everywhere the merriment of the approaching Noel seemed to reign supreme.

For Aria, the center of her own communal experience was the little church that was situated on a small parcel of land across from the post office and an antique store downtown. Most of the commercial traffic ran along the county highway so this area of the Crossroads— (as the townsfolk referred to it)—was relatively quiet and calm, as if the town had moved on, leaving the old relics of what it had once been behind. Like a dry corn husk or a butterfly's chrysalis. Irrelevant or enduringly charming, depending upon your point of view.

Even quieter now, Anderson's Crossroads was blanketed in snow, while still more flakes fluttered down like ash, the streets empty and glistening under the sodium streetlights. Looming above, the sky was the silver-gray of a wolf's pelt, the wind stirring up little drifts of snow and sending them spinning like mischievous winter sprites. An almost silent night, the only sound coming from beyond the golden glow of windows at the little church.

Aria Chambers was inside that little church on that evening three days before Christmas, cocooned within her wool sweater, seated on the end of the pew, second row from last. Her customary spot. Tonight was the children's program and then Christmas Eve would have the adult choir'. Currently, the little singers were attempting to work their way through "O Holy Night," while a frazzled Natalie Fassbinder—who also taught children's church—held up flashcards to help guide the little carolers along, never mind that half of them couldn't read and the other half were distracted by the smiling congregants or their peers.

The children weren't the only ones distracted. Aria had the old letter in her hand, tears welling in her eyes that somehow she had been able to hold back for the time being by no small measure of self-control. Her gaze moved to the windows. It was that deep dark of winter, but she could see little flakes of snow flitting against the window like scattered sand. The snow used to be such a comfort for her—such a *joy*—reminding her of winters past. Now, the season seemed to simply exacerbate the ache inside her heart in the same way that the bitter chill could get under your clothes and stab at your skin with a thousand little probing needles. Her favorite season was also a reminder of profound loss.

It's been two years, she thought. *Time to let it go.* Two Christmases, burdened by grief, days that had become more bitter than jolly. But letting go was something easier said than done. Loss was not just a vacuum that left a profound emptiness behind...it sucked everything living into that emptiness like a black hole. Two years removed, the tragic event had happened the week before Christmas, on a snowy night just like this one.

The letter was a reminder of what had been left behind. What had been lost. Never mind that she had stacks and stacks of letters that her beloved David had written over the years, all tucked away in a box in her closet. This one was the one that mattered the most because this was the last one, the final reminder that he was gone forever. In the end, this one was the only one that really mattered.

She hadn't been there when they pulled his car out of the freezing lake. Black ice and a howling wind had conspired against her fiancé's car to sweep it off the side of a bridge in upstate New York. He had been coming home to see her for Christmas break. Just a few days at her parents' home, the rare reprieve that they had managed to steal away between semesters, he as a student at Syracuse and her at University of Missouri. Seeing him was really the only thing that Aria wanted that Christmas, and when she had asked him to make the trip he had agreed, not letting the treacherous night keep him from trying to make his flight out of LaGuardia. By the following Christmas—last year—they would be married. At least that had been the plan.

The letter was a somber reminder that even life's fondest plans could be unmade. The letter had been sent out a week before David's scheduled flight and had arrived the day before the accident. Aria could still remember retrieving it from the mailbox and tearing it open. Reading it as fast as she could before holding it against her chest like she was some kind of Jane Austen character or something...silly and in love and mindless of what anyone else might have thought. Their love was a fairy tale, but overnight that romantic story of their lives together would become a tragedy.

It was David's idea to exchange letters while they were away from each other, an old-fashioned but welcome idea. At least one letter a week, that was their rule. Sure, they would text each other and call and all that good stuff but the letters were special. Reminders of true love that they could hold onto forever. Something *tangible.* Aria had thought then she would show them to their children someday, that they in turn might hold onto them long after Aria was gone as artifacts of affection.

She had gotten a little stronger in the past two years, and she guessed that was progress. But it didn't mean she was ready to find someone new. Not that that stopped the church folks from trying to set her up with this nephew or that friend. Everyone fancied themselves a matchmaker, as if a lady couldn't just exist by herself for a while. She wasn't ready...that was it, that was the simple fact of it all. Besides that, there weren't too many prospects even if she *was* inclined to put herself back out there on the market. *Ugh...as if I'm a heifer at the livestock exchange.* That brought a smile to her face at least. *Wonder what the going rate is for a single girl in her mid-twenties?*

Anderson's Crossroads had a population of a few thousand, but her church only had around thirty on an average Sunday morning. A farming community, the Crossroads used to be a major trading post. All that remained of the town's heydays was a livestock exchange that drew a modest out-of-town crowd on the weekend and a mill where almost all of the Crossroads' working class received their salary. The rest of the sleepy town's denizens were retired folk and children.

The chorus finished on a particularly ear-splitting crescendo of the classic hymn and now one of the little girls from the children's choir was stepping up on a stool so that she could recite a poem into the microphone affixed to the podium. Aria was reminded of the fact that Pastor Gillman didn't ever seem to need that microphone at all...his deep, booming vibrato had no lack of amplification, especially when certain segments of a sermon demanded extra emphasis. For that matter, the sound man didn't even turn it on during Sunday morning services unless there was a musical special scheduled.

The little girl leaning up toward the microphone brought another smile to Aria's face. She folded the letter up and slipped it back into her purse. Folding her arms over her chest she turned her attention back to the program.

After the service there were cookies, hot chocolate, and other sugary confections on display in the fellowship hall. Most everyone shuffled over there after the closing prayer and either stood milling about the coffee maker or finding a seat at one of the tables. It reminded her of the reception after David's funeral. It seemed that bereavement poisoned every festive moment, pulling her thoughts helplessly back to his death like a migratory bird back home. She supposed that there might always be remnants of his life scattered throughout every moment of her life, a shadow forever cast by the sun. The most innocuous things like sad souvenirs of a life cut way too short: The Baskin-Robbins where they had shared their first ice cream cone; Mistletoe, under which they'd jostle one another, giggling; White hoodies, his casual apparel of choice (and which she borrowed more often than he even got to wear them himself). A million reminders, each providing a little stab of pain.

In defiance of the residue of sadness that clung to her, Aria selected a couple sugar cookies, and a cup of hot chocolate and took her seat over by Ralph Schaeffer, who taught the adults' Sunday school class, and his wife Eva. The happy couple always seemed to provide a joyful distraction.

"So," Eva said, her eyes sparkling. "What do you have planned for Christmas, dear? Going to see your folks?"

Aria shook her head. Her parents lived in Portland. "Not this year I'm afraid, though I think they're planning a trip out here in the spring. Still working on paying back student loans I'm afraid, so I don't really have enough for something so extravagant as a trip to Oregon."

"Well, that would be nice if they could make it," Eva mused. "Of course, you're always welcome to come over to our house. I'm planning on making a nice meal: Meatloaf, mashed potatoes and all the trimmings to go with it."

"Oh, thanks so much!" Aria replied. "But I think I'm going to have a small thing at my place. Me and the cat." *You sound utterly pathetic,* she thought to herself, smiling. *Are you really ready to play the role of lonely old cat lady?*

"Ok, hon...just keep it in mind, won't you?"

Aria nodded, reaching out and giving Eva's hand a gentle squeeze. "Thank you again. Really."

Eva waved her away. "Think nothing of it. You know you're like a daughter to us."

That's what Aria loved about her church: Everyone was family, and everybody seemed to look out for one another. *Like a church family should,* Ralph would say emphatically. She often compared this congregation to her "real" family, marveling at how much turbulence the Chambers had endured over the years. Sometimes it was better when there was a little distance between them, as sad as that might be for her to admit. Especially around the holidays, when she could use that support system. It wasn't that she couldn't count on the church people to help guide her through the darkness, it was just that it seemed a little different. Too many times there were people nearby ready to help—people like Eva, Ralph, and the pastor—it was just that she didn't want to unload her burdens upon them so she usually just struggled under its weight herself. At the same time, it was best to have a little distance between herself and her family...not a division so much as a necessary buffer. Especially with her brother, Marcus, who seemed to be constantly getting into trouble and asking for money. She felt guilty keeping him at an arm's length—she truly loved him, of course—but whatever social and financial troubles he had, Aria was afraid it might be contagious. He was fun and likeable in so many ways, but he also tended to drag people down with him. Life was already heavy enough for Aria without that added weight, though she did feel almost constantly guilty about the distance that was growing between them. *When was the last time you two even talked?* She wondered to herself. It was a question that she couldn't answer right away.

Her house was a couple blocks away and Aria had decided to walk to the special holiday service. An hour or so ago that meant a gentle drift of snowfall was coming down, puffy fat flakes falling from the heavens...the perfect ambiance to an enchanted holiday evening. Since then, it had accumulated, the snow now several inches deep, enough to obscure the sidewalk and roads. Everything was covered in a cold white carpet and by the look of things it wasn't going to relent any time soon. The temperature had dropped a little, also, though the chill in the air wasn't unpleasant.

As the fellowship wound down and people started to cautiously pull out from the church parking lot, Aria said her goodbyes and ventured out into the night. (This involved turning down rides from just about everyone, but she liked the thought of walking by herself, alone to decipher her own thoughts in a winter wonderland).

She found that she was forced to walk on the road itself—she couldn't see the sidewalk and didn't want to plunge through the snow accidentally and fall into a ditch. That was just fine because there were no cars on the road now that everyone had evacuated the church and the last of the taillights were receding into the pale night. The snow nestled everything into its silent embrace, creating a vast expanse of endless white as if transporting Aria into a pristine and otherworldly kingdom. The sky was deepening to a darker gray, the only thing that moved in the night the gently descending flakes and the single stoplight flashing red in a monotonous cycle, keeping sentinel over the old downtown area.

Everything was so quiet now that Aria could hear her own breath coming in and out, the light crunch of her footsteps in the snow. Vapor floated up through the air like little manufactured clouds. The snowfall continued unabated, and judging by the scene Aria figured that Anderson's Crossroads was in for at least several inches more. *There will be snow on the ground for Christmas,* she thought to herself and smiled. *The first white Christmas in...what?...three years?*

It was amazing how a little snow around the holidays could lighten her mood. The letter, folded up in her purse, was for now just a vague memory, her thoughts fixed on more joyous musings: the candlelight service tomorrow night, Christmas itself, starting a fire in the hearth and maybe boiling some water for hot cocoa. She might even try to find one of the many iterations of *A Christmas Carol* on TV, experience Scrooge's fateful night for the umpteenth time.

Ah, that story never gets old, does it? It did not. *You're feeling much better now, aren't you?* She was. *Just walkin' in a winter wonderland.*

The smile on her face faltered. She stopped abruptly, her breath catching in her throat. When she breathed again a moment later the condensation sent a cloud out in front of her, obscuring her view for a moment. As foolish children she remembered her and her brother breaking off twigs and pretending to use them as cigars, the cold breath like smoke. She was breathing a little more rapidly now, but far from imagining anything so familiar or pleasant.

Across the road stood her house, a three-bedroom Victorian painted white with black shutters and a gabled roof, the façade almost invisible now behind the veil of falling snow. But what *was* visible was a light shining from the second story window. She tried to remember how she'd forgotten to turn it off. Then it occurred to her that she *hadn't* forgotten...she never forgot. It was a habit that had become as second nature as flushing the toilet, an automatic response instilled from her youth by parents—her father, in particular—that would never cease to lament about the toll that lazy habits levied upon climbing energy bills.

She stared up at it, wondering, the blazing light as alien as a specter, her hands stuffed in the pockets of her coat. She cocked her head as if attempting to dislodge a memory like a candy bar stuck in a vending machine, trying to get it all to make sense, simply because she didn't want to consider the alternative...the unthinkable: That someone else had, in fact, turned it on.

Then she saw a shadow pass over the window upstairs and a moment later the light was extinguished.

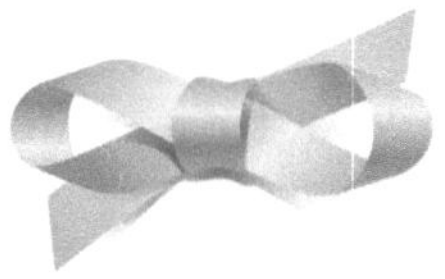

TWO

Aria stood frozen in place, staring at the darkened house. Slowly, she reached into her purse and extracted her cellphone. With fingers trembling from a mixture of cold and the fear creeping down her spine like melted ice, she dialed 911. A moment later there was a voice on the other line.

"911, can I help you?"

"Hi...uh...I think someone is in my house."

A pause. "Okay...and to whom am I speaking?"

Flustered, Aria said: "Sorry...it's Aria Chambers. I live at 108 Sycamore..."

"Okay. And did I hear you correctly, you think you have an intruder in your home...is that right?"

"Yes, yes, that's right."

"Please retreat to a safe distance and we'll send someone out as soon as possible."

"Thanks so much," Aria said, nervously glancing at the house. "Please hurry."

"I have someone enroute, but please stay on the line."

Aria stood there, phone in hand, gaze flitting from one blank window to the next.

Only a couple minutes had passed before Aria spied the cruiser plowing through the snow like a sled dog, heading in her direction, the red and blue lights spinning and casting soft pastel colors onto the snow. She stood patiently on the invisible sidewalk, her hands plunged deep in her coat pockets, her breath coming in shallow, frequent exhalations. The snow crunched under the cruiser's tires as the officer slowly pulled alongside her. A moment later the driver got out, placing a hat delicately on his head.

Aria shook her head in wonderment. "*Trevor?*" She asked. "Trevor Mason?"

"The one and only," he responded with a boyish smile. Temporarily, they had both forgotten the reason for this unexpected reunion. "Sorry if you were expecting someone else..."

She laughed, but out here in the cold and in the midst of the frightful situation for which he had been summoned, it sounded a bit hollow. Not that she meant it to. She was simply surprised. No, more than surprised, she was absolutely flabbergasted. "How long has it been?" She asked.

His eyebrows arched and he sucked some air between teeth gritted against the cold. "Five years? No...maybe it's been six. Can that be right? You went to vet school, if I remember correctly; I was behind you two years and then had college and the academy."

"That's right. Yeah, I'm a vet now working for—"

"Peter Dillahunt."

"That's right," Aria said, then gave him a coy, sidelong glance. "Have you been stalking me?"

Sheepishly, Trevor shook his head vigorously side to side. "No, no, of course not. I just..." Aria thought that he had turned even more pale now, and she actually felt bad that her attempt at a little light flirting had caused him so much embarrassment.

"Well," she said, shifting uncomfortably on her feet before looking over her shoulder at the still, dark house. "Maybe we can catch up some time. I called because there is someone in my house. I saw a shadow—a figure, upstairs in the window—and then the light went out."

Trevor looked past her, his gaze drifting upwards. For now, nothing in the old house moved. *Not a creature stirring, not even a murderous intruder,* Aria thought, following his gaze. Now she was the one to be embarrassed. Whoever had been up there could have slipped out the back door and might already be trudging through the neighbor's yard, disappearing into the night. But Aria had that ominous feeling that the perpetrator *was* still in there somewhere, maybe peering out through a window at them right now. Waiting until the police officer left so he could get her alone. *But what could he possibly want with me?*

The various possibilities that might answer that question danced through her head with maniacal glee, unsettling her even more. None of the options she could come up with were good ones, so she tried to shove the whole silent slideshow out of her mind completely. For his part, Trevor seemed to sense the return of that cold, frightening spirit, because he gave her a reassuring nod before moving past her. "I'll check it out," he said. "Do you want to sit in the patrol car where it's warm?"

"Not on your life," Aria said, shivering, the wintry chill a finger that traced down her spine like a skeletal caress. "I'm going with you."

He shot her a glance. "I don't think that—"

"I've seen my share of horror movies," Aria said. "I'm not staying out here alone, and I'm certainly not going to sit in an unmanned police car waiting for the boogeyman to come back out here and get me."

Trevor examined her before offering a little shrug and moving toward where the front walk would be if it hadn't been rubbed away by the accumulating snow. "Suit yourself," he whispered. There was a snap of something being unbuttoned and suddenly he had his service pistol in both hands. Together, they crept up the front steps of the house.

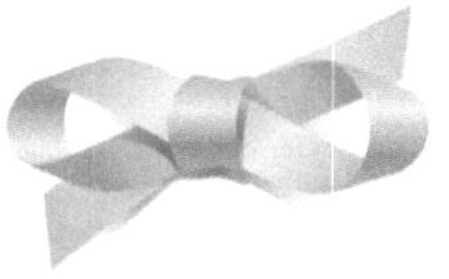

THREE

She pulled open the creaking screen door, but the front door was locked, so Aria fumbled with her keys—her nerves and gloved hands making the whole operation a cumbersome one—finally managing to select the right one. Slowly, she twisted it in the lock, her fingers trembling. There was a click, and then she was easing the creaking door open. Trevor brushed by her, gun protruding into the gloom as he started to clear the room. Aria stayed huddled just behind him, her eyes scanning the shadows for any sign of the intruder.

Beyond the alcove was a short hallway that gave way to the kitchen on the right. To their immediate left was a staircase. Swiftly, Trevor moved to the right, sliding through the living room smoothly between the couch and end table and the TV. There was a second entranceway to the kitchen on that side, Aria's small dining room table separating it from the living room.

Aria lingered near the front door, which was now standing open. She could feel the cold breath of the winter night seeping through the thin glass of the screen door. Silently, she waited as Trevor—*Officer Mason,* she corrected herself—moved out of sight, disappearing into the kitchen.

Aria's gaze drifted toward the staircase that stretched up into the darkness. In the silence, she could feel her heart beating a steady cadence, the rush of blood discernible in her ears. *Please, Lord,* she prayed. *Keep us both safe.*

A moment later Trevor appeared in the hallway, having emerged from the kitchen with the gun still held firmly in both hands. He glanced out the back door window, then crept toward her. He gave her a little shake of the head, then whispered, "It's clear down here."

Aria nodded encouragingly.

As if on cue, there was a creaking of boards from somewhere above, and two sets of eyes drifted toward the ceiling before exchanging a concerned glance. Trevor gave her a reassuring nod and then turned toward the stairs. Aria rushed to keep up, one hand on the back of his coat. Though it seemed they would be heading right toward the danger, the thought of being left alone on the ground floor terrified her even more than the possible confrontation.

As he mounted the stairs, Trevor's fur-lined coat made a gentle swishing sound. Aria found herself grabbing hold of the material more tightly, staying right on his heels as he climbed the stairs. She felt a little ridiculous holding onto him like that, but she also felt secure, as if she was sure that he wouldn't let any harm befall her.

They climbed the stairs slowly, trying to keep every sound—the whisper of a board under their weight, the gentle swish of fabric—at a minimum. This, Aria sensed, was both so that they could maintain the advantage of surprise and also to be able to try and track the intruder's position. They reached the little landing, turned, and started up the last set of stairs that would take them to the second floor and wherever the intruder might be hiding. *He's waiting up here for us,* Aria thought, feeling a sudden chill pass over her.

She tried to focus on the silence, but still those frantic thoughts plagued her. *What if he's armed? What if I've just called Trevor to go marching to his death?* She was concerned for her safety, and there was even this little hint of...*What?* She asked herself, surprising herself by this sudden concern: that she hadn't even gotten a chance to become reacquainted with him after all these years. Here he was right now, an evolution of that gawky kid she'd last seen in high school five or six years ago. He'd changed—for the better, at least as far as what she'd seen up to this point. He was handsome, tall, and seemed a lot more confident than he'd been before. He'd grown into his skin, and she was seeing him anew—or, perhaps, really only seeing him for the first time now. The fact that he'd had a crush on her way back then wasn't exactly a big secret over the years, but she had overlooked him then. Now it seemed impossible that she hadn't ever really considered him in any kind of romantic way. But David had come along around then, too, she reminded herself.

All that didn't matter right now, of course, and Aria felt silly—even selfish, truth be told—that she was even giving her thoughts any space to ruminate over such matters when they were both stepping into the gaping mouth of danger. She needed to be alert and helpful, not daydreaming about some romantic fantasy.

They finally reached the second floor without incident, but also with no clearer understanding of where the stranger that had broken into the house might be lurking. Trevor seemed unsure which side of the house's second story to start with first.

Aria gave him a little nudge, guiding him to the left. After all, that's where she'd seen the shadow. He glanced at her and she shrugged, as if to say: *We have to start somewhere, right?*

He nodded, whispering: "Watch my back, okay? Just in case."

Aria nodded furiously. Behind them were three closed doors, one leading to the hallway bathroom and the other two to bedrooms, one of which had been converted into a study/ storage room. The stranger could be hiding in one of those rooms, but with the doors being closed at least that possibility didn't present a clear and present danger.

Trevor continued forward, the wan light of the moon and a solitary streetlight providing just enough illumination to cast a discernible path before them. The master bedroom was coming up on the left, and even now Aria could see that the door was cracked open an inch or two.

Did you leave it open?

She couldn't remember, and trying to decide now would be nothing more than hazarding a guess. The master bedroom was where she slept, the adjoining full bathroom where she got ready every day. Right now, the stranger being up here anywhere was a violation of her security. She had heard of people getting robbed—or worse—and how the survivor never quite feels safe ever again. Aria wondered if she'd already lost that sense of security...if it was, indeed, gone for good, no matter how the events of the next few minutes turned out.

She tried to keep such thoughts at bay. *You must stay alert. Both your life and now Trevor's depends upon your vigilance. Don't let him down!*

Trevor reached the door to the master bedroom. He paused, shot her a look as if to ask permission to enter that sacred realm, and Aria nodded. He took a breath, nudged the door open with the back of his left hand, the other cradling the gun. With a long, shrill creak that seemed deafening in the silence, the master bedroom door slowly withdrew. Beyond the threshold lay only darker shadows.

If this had been the last room they'd come to then Officer Trevor Mason would have called out a warning. Often times it was that sense of authority—the command of words spoken in confidence—that would get the job done, bringing bad guys into subjection. Of course, that didn't always work. However, since this was only the first room upstairs that they were about to enter, Trevor didn't think it really was the best option because they hadn't checked the other rooms on this floor yet, and giving up their position didn't seem like the best course of action. The element of surprise was an advantage he was not in a hurry to surrender. Not yet anyways. Instead, he opted for stealth, not speaking a word as he slipped wraithlike into the room.

Aria was right behind him, her eyes momentarily looking over her shoulder in case someone chose that very moment to sneak up on them from the gloom and try to overtake them. The hallway was barren and still.

The darkness was so deep that Aria wondered now how she had ever found it acceptable to sleep with the lights out at night, all alone in this big house. A voice in her mind—one that seemed very despairing, as if lamenting the loss of the last vestige of innocence—whispered that she would indeed never be able to just surrender to the darkness of night again. That the feeling of security had indeed been forever lost. That she would, from this moment forward, always wonder if there was someone else in the room with her.

She fought against that susceptibility. *I won't live the life of a coward,* she promised herself, watching as Trevor continued to inch forward, seemingly committed to sharing the creed himself. *No matter what happens.* A moment later he was in the center of the room, standing there as he guided the barrel of the gun around the room, probing at shadows. Aria was at his back, waiting for what—if anything—might come next. Allowing every sense at their command to become intimately attuned to their surroundings. Immersing themselves in this new atmosphere like astronauts acclimating themselves to a new and unfamiliar planet.

Then they heard something—the sound of plastic scraping, perhaps—and they both shot a glance in the direction of the bathroom, the door facing them like a pale and resolute barrier. Aria knew what that unmistakable sound was: Someone drawing back the shower curtain. Trevor gave Aria an uncertain glance and she just looked back at him, blinking. She thought she heard another sound in that moment—the sole of a shoe squeaking ever-so-lightly against the tiles.

Trevor held out one palm, the fingers of his hand spread out. *Don't move.* Then he lifted that same hand and held an index finger to his lips. *Don't make a sound.* Creeping forward, he squeezed the pistol tighter in his right hand, angling it down at the midsection of the door. Waist high. With his free hand he slowly reached toward the knob. With agonizing care, he slipped his hand around the knob, gripping it with his fingers, and gave Aria one last look. Nodding, he braced himself and then slowly turned it. A moment later he shoved forced the door inward.

Someone rushed out of the gloom, a banshee cry piercing the silence. Trevor ducked a little, bringing his free hand back to brace the gun. Whoever had been crouching in the bathroom barreled into Trevor, knocking him off-balance and stumbling to one side. Aria crouched, tried to get out of the intruder's way. Groaning, Trevor tracked the other man with the gun, his finger dancing across the trigger. The perpetrator was moving between them, directly toward the bed. Reflexively, Trevor kicked out a leg just in time and caught the stranger by the shin. The intruder cried out, falling, and tumbled onto the bed.

"Freeze!" Trevor shouted loudly, leaning on one knee as he peered down the barrel pointed at the stranger's head. "Don't move unless you want me to ventilate your skull."

The stranger rolled over onto his back, then scurried like a frightened mouse toward the headboard. Aria hurried forward, reaching for the light switch, and flipping it on. Immediately the bedroom brightened, the shadows dispelled into the night.

Aria blinked, her chest heaving and her mouth gaping open. "M-M-Marcus?" She stammered. "What...what are you doing here?"

Trevor remained where he was, frozen like a statue, the gun still aimed at the intruder. But he was looking back confusedly at Aria. "You...you know him?"

Aria laughed, relief flooding through her as she shook her head in disbelief. "Yeah, I'd say so. He's my brother."

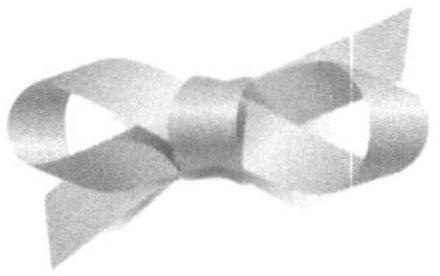

FOUR

They were in the living room, Aria pacing back and forth as Officer Mason stood nearby with his thumbs hitched in his belt. Marcus was sitting on the couch, leaning forward with his fingers interlaced, staring at the carpet. A swath of hair obscured his face, but it was apparent that he was very embarrassed. Though the fears of who might have been lurking inside the house had been allied, the intruder identified, the tension still hung palpably in the air.

"The big question I have," Aria said, folding her arms as she looked at her brother. "Is how did you get in here? The door was locked, and—"

Marcus Chambers gave her a sheepish look. "Yeah, I tried the front door and the back one as well. It's good you kept them locked. The ground floor windows were locked, but the one in the bedroom—your bedroom. Well..."

"But Marcus, that's on the second floor."

He spread his hands, as if saying: *Where there's a will there's a way.*

A beat passed then Aria blurted: "Wait...you climbed up the rain spout?"

Marcus looked away, not offering a response.

Letting out a pent-up breath, Trevor shook his head before deciding to enter the fray. "I can't tell you how close you came to being shot. I guess I don't know why you would just come bursting out of the bathroom like that. This evening could have ended much differently. You easily could have been killed."

Marcus nodded, running his fingers through his hair. "I know, I know. Maybe that would have been better."

"Marcus," Aria interrupted. "Don't talk like that."

"Sorry. It's just that..." He looked away. "Well, I'm in some pretty serious trouble."

Aria frowned, crossing her arms over her chest. "What are you talking about? What kind of trouble? Are you..."

He shot her a look, but there was none of the arrogance of the younger Marcus Chambers in it—the confident, athletic kid she'd grown up with. Instead, it was more a look of suspicion mingled with paranoia. Like Marcus was desperate to either find someone he could trust or at least to know where he stood. The helplessness and desperation caused something inside Aria to jar loose, threatening to break her heart anew. *I've already lost David...I can't lose him, too. No matter what he's done.*

The silence stretched out, giving brother and sister adequate time to fill it with unspoken questions and words. Months—maybe even years—of regrets tumbling recklessly through their minds. All those unspoken words into the ether, like cleaning out the rooms of some forlorn and crumbling house.

"Look," Marcus said, his brow furrowing as he examined his restless hands. "I don't know if I can say that I'm clean or not. I cannot say that one hundred percent because it's been...it hasn't been that long since I last used. But I've been one hundred percent *trying*...I can say that truthfully. I've been going to my meetings just as regular as clockwork...I promise. It just..." he looked away, and in that moment Aria saw something so vulnerable—a flash of an expression that was so boyish...a reflection of childhood. "It keeps somehow reeling me back in. That sounds lame, I know—just a typical junkie's excuse. But this time...well, this time it's more like some*ones*—not some*things*—are pulling on me. It's different this time—not all up to me, and I can't change it even if I want to. If I can't escape the presence of that poison what chance do I have?"

"I don't understand everything you're telling me," Aria said, reaching out for his hand. "So, I'll reserve judgment. But explain it to me, okay? Are you saying that there are people after you?"

Marcus glanced at Trevor, as if seeing the police officer for the first time. Then his gaze shifted to Aria. "You can talk," she said. "This is Officer Mason—Trevor—and he's a friend. We...Marcus, we just want to help."

Trevor cleared his throat. "I know that you don't know me, but your sister is right. Help us get a handle on this. Help us know what trouble you're in—and who it is your involved with, and we'll see what we can do about it."

Marcus took a deep, shuddering breath. "I wish you could help...I really do. I tried going to the cops in Omaha. No disrespect, man, but that didn't help at all. In fact, it only made things worse. These are dangerous, deadly, very *bad* people involved with this and their network has a reach like an octopus. It's..." Frustrated, Marcus just shook his head. "There's nothing you can do to help. Besides, I don't want to drag my sister—any of my family—into it. That's why I just snuck into the house. I just need...man, I'm so tired...I just need to hide out for a few days, get a little sleep."

Aria leaned forward. "Marcus, you know you can stay here as long as you need to. I've just had one big rule you have to abide by, and I don't need to tell you what that one thing is."

Marcus nodded. "No drugs. No alcohol. Yeah, I know, sis, and I'm really thankful for the help. But I feel like wherever I am danger is going to follow me like a shadow. I could never forgive myself if anything was to happen to you, especially if I was the direct cause of it."

"I'm committed to making sure that Aria stays safe," Trevor said. "Let's help you sort this stuff out, huh? Keep you safe also."

Marcus didn't say anything, but Aria knew that saying her brother would be hesitant to accept any help from the boys in blue was the understatement of the century. Her brother's past as far as law enforcement was concerned was one of mutual distrust and apprehension. Problematic, to say the least. Still, there had to be some middle ground here.

"Why don't you at least stay the night here?" Aria asked. "You can get some rest then you can move on if you want. Or we can try and help get whoever is behind this off your back. It's your choice. Trevor is a police officer, he—"

"I wouldn't want *him* to get hurt either," Marcus said. "And I'm afraid that is exactly what will happen." Suddenly, he scooted his chair back and got to his feet. "When you weren't home and I saw all the lights out I figured you went to Mom and Dad's for the holidays. I'm sorry I exposed you to any danger."

"What danger?" Aria asked in frustration, standing also now. "Who's going to bother you in a little town like Anderson's Crossroads?"

He smirked a little, though the fear never left his eyes. Then he cast his gaze toward the front door as if half expecting these unnamed boogeymen would come crashing through it at any moment. "They'll keep coming after me until they find me. Until they...silence me."

Aria shook her head. "Just keep your head low, stay here for a little while. They won't—"

"Aria!" Marcus said, more insistently now. "You have no idea who these guys are...what they're capable of. You gotta let what I'm saying sink in! They're coming, they won't be stopped, and I don't want anyone who I care about to be caught in the crossfire."

"But how do you know..."

Marcus sighed. He walked across the room and slunk down on the couch. "Look, I drove out of Omaha yesterday afternoon. When I reached North Platte I grabbed some lunch and when I started to come out of the restaurant these two sketchy looking dudes were snooping around my car. They didn't see me so I snuck out the back. For once I caught a lucky break—there was a Greyhound nearby and I jumped on the next bus. There's only a couple towns between North Platte and Anderson's Crossroads so the likelihood that they're heading this way is pretty much a sure thing. Plus..." Marcus grabbed a throw pillow and stuffed his face into it. For a moment Aria thought he might scream into it, but after a moment he removed it and tossed it aside, leaning back and staring at the ceiling. "Like I said, I made a big mistake coming here. They're going to know that I have a sister that lives here in this town and they'll assume that I came this way. Man, I really screwed up big..."

"Marcus," Trevor said. "Who are these guys? Is there anything—anything at all—you can tell us about them that will help?"

Marcus considered that, then shook his head slowly side to side. "I wish I could, man, but this is way bigger than you and I. It's something I've gotta run from because facing these guys would be a suicide mission."

It took them a few hours but Aria and Trevor were finally able to get Marcus to settle down just a little bit—enough, at least, for him to be convinced to remain in Anderson's Crossings for the night. There was, after all, no reason to try and drive through the blizzard that seemed to be slowly unfolding around them.

The plan was simple, the best they could do on short notice: Trevor had decided that he would take both Aria and Marcus to his great grandmother's house, sitting vacant due to the fact that Ms. Olivia Mason was currently a resident at Majestic Pines Nursing Care Facility in North Platte.

"You all can hunker down there tonight—or really for however long you need."

Aria was overcome by gratitude. "Trevor, you've done so much already."

"Nonsense. I've only done my job. Besides, I would never forgive myself if something happened to either of you."

Grudgingly, Marcus had agreed. He jumped into the passenger seat of Aria's Honda and they followed Officer Mason through the thick curtain of snow the half mile it took to Ms. Mason's house.

"Make yourself at home," Marcus said.

"Easy for you to say," Aria winked at him. "Are you sure that your grandma would be okay with a bunch of strangers descending upon her lovely home?"

Marcus shrugged. "What she doesn't know won't hurt her."

Aria went to slug him in the shoulder and he grinned at her, pulling away.

"I'm just kidding," Marcus said. "I lived here with her before we had to put her in a facility. She has one of the most generous hearts of anyone that I know. I wish she could still be in her home but she's got some serious medical issues that required the professionals to take over her care."

"Do you see her regularly?" Aria asked. "I would think it would get lonely being in one of those places."

"Once a week," Trevor said. "Granny Mason is the reason why I decided to stay here in this little town." Dropping his head, he continued: "She's gotten worse in the last few months. She's ninety-three, though. Sometimes she doesn't even seem to recognize me, and even then she's only half there it seems."

"I'm sorry," Aria said.

"Well," Trevor said, attempting to change the subject. "Let's get you all situated. Marcus, there's a bedroom in the back west corner of the house that I think you'll find suitable enough. Aria, if you'd like you can take the guest room over here..."

Marcus gave them the brief tour, including where to find towels and washcloths if either of them wanted to take a shower. He showed them the kitchen, apologizing for the fact that the pantry had only limited supplies. Still, there were Pop-tarts and oatmeal in abundance, as well as bottles of water and juice. He retrieved fresh sheets for Aria and asked them if they needed anything else.

"I think I'm set," Marcus said, yawning. "And I'm dead tired. Not sure how far I'd have made it through this snow, so thanks so much."

"Don't mention it," Trevor replied.

"I'm going to hit the sack, then," Marcus said.

As he left, Trevor and Aria stood awkwardly together in the living room. Trying to figure out how far back in the past they'd have to retrace in order to catch up again. After a moment, Aria said: "You sure have changed since I last saw you. Not in a bad way, either. I mean...well, you're bigger, older..."

He chuckled. "Not a kid anymore?"

"Well..." Aria was at a loss.

"It was a matter of time before we ran into each other again," Trevor observed. "Though there for a while I wasn't sure you'd come back after heading off to college."

"Neither did my parents," Aria said. "They thought they could count on me going down to Arizona. 'You can get a job as a vet just about anywhere,' Mom said. Guess she's right."

"Then why Anderson's Crossroads? Why not Arizona...or Omaha, for that matter? What made you want to stay *here*?"

Aria shrugged. "The easy answer is that this is home. I'm not ready to leave just yet, even if it was to go to Omaha or somewhere else nearby. Uproot myself. It's my church. The people. The old familiar things that are so hard to let go of."

Trevor nodded. "Guess I can't disagree with you. I mean, that's basically what I did."

"My time is going to come, and very soon I suspect," Aria said. "Peter Dillahunt—the vet—is the best, but I didn't spend all this time and take out all these loans to be a Vet Assistant. Soon, I'm going to have to either start my own clinic or find a position in a bigger city."

"Understandable. Though I'm sure everyone here would hate to see you go."

Aria shrugged. "Perhaps." She looked at him and offered a smile. "What about you? You don't want to be out there on the busy streets of a big city busting the bad guys? Is the small-town life good enough for you?"

He nodded, thoughtful. "As you know, I grew up here as well and I know exactly what you mean. When I was a kid I couldn't wait to leave Anderson's Crossroads, but now that I'm older I can't imagine living anywhere else."

"I get that."

Trevor continued: "For me it really is about protecting and serving. Man, that sounds really cringey, doesn't it? I mean to say that I do find police work very interesting, but I'll leave all the gunfights and car chases to the movies. I go to the Baptist church here in town. It's a small congregation—about twenty-five on an average Sunday—but those folks are family. And with Granny Olivia nearby..." He let the words drift away, the silence self-explanatory.

Aria regarded him for a moment. "I'm surprised that it took us so long to run into each other again. It really has been a long time, hasn't it?"

"Too long." The words were out of his mouth before he stopped himself. He blushed a little, turning away.

"Thank you," Aria said. "For everything. I wish we could have gotten reacquainted under entirely different circumstances, but I'm very grateful for all you did for me and my brother tonight."

"It's my pleasure," he responded. "I just want you two to stay safe and hopefully get some rest."

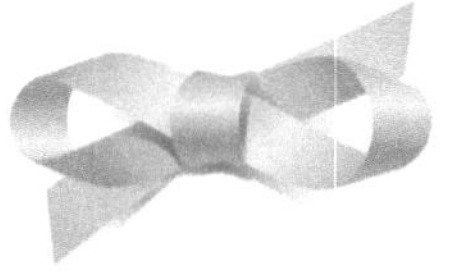

December 23rd

FIVE

Aria awoke feeling a little disoriented. She tried to mentally recalibrate herself, retracing the steps that led her to this unfamiliar bed. As the events of the previous evening reestablished themselves from memory, she looked around the room and just soaked in the silence for a while. Everything was still, the room cozy and warm. Outside, the restless snowstorm had abated, and now there was little more than a powdery residue drifting down, almost too light to be seen. She felt refreshed, more optimistic in the growing morning light.

Kicking off the covers, she slipped out of the warm bed and onto the cold floor, venturing out of the guest room and into the hallway. The door to the bedroom in which Marcus had slept stood cracked open a foot, but Aria went in without knocking, searching for her brother. Hearing nothing immediately, she reversed course to the room where she fetched an overnight bag and then hunted down some of the towels that Trevor said could be found in the hallway closet right outside the bathroom.

The hot stream of water flowed over her, reinvigorating, and refreshing. It seemed to melt away the anxiety of the previous night. When she emerged fifteen minutes later, reawakened, she thought she just might be halfway prepared to meet the challenges of the day. She began to form a mental checklist...a plan of attack. Even then, she considered that perhaps her brother might have been driven more by paranoia than cold facts and actual threats. She wondered if maybe the new day would also provide him a new outlook.

After drying and getting dressed in clothes she'd hastily packed before she took her exodus from her own home the night before, she pulled a brush through her hair as she roamed through the house looking for Marcus. Calling out his name, she ventured first into the living room, then dining room, then kitchen. She spotted a bowl and spoon in the sink. Turning, she gazed back toward his bedroom, a tightness in her stomach.

He was nowhere to be found. He was not in the bedroom, though the bed appeared hastily made, neither was he found in the bathroom. Her stomach tightened even more as she began to come to grips with the possibility that he had left town, though she wasn't sure how he'd manage to accomplish that task without a vehicle. Then she spotted something near the headboard, a wrapped gift resting between the pillows.

She ventured closer, picking up the gift in her hands. Wrapped in dollar store paper and with an adhesive-backed bow attached, it had all the signs of her brother's thoughtful though amateurish handiwork. There was even a makeshift tag beneath the bow: *TO: ARIA. FROM: MARCUS. MERRY CHRISMAS.* ("Christmas" was misspelled).

She stood there for a moment, first staring at the gift and then out the window. For some reason the first emotion that flooded inside was an unfathomable sadness. The room suddenly felt very empty and she felt very alone. Like he was already a thousand miles away, which might very well be close to the truth. The alternative was too much to consider, so she brushed that away. Then she opened up the gift.

Inside was a large container of perfume, an opaque bottle rimmed in aqua blue. A note had been taped to the backside. She pulled off the cap, positioning the atomizer over her wrist and pressing down twice. She rubbed her wrists together and smelled the fragrance as she examined the handwritten note. Steeling herself, she finally gave it a closer look.

Little Sis—

I hope you have a Merry Christmas. It was so good to see you again, even under these circumstances. You are such a buietiful person—I've known that for a very long time now, even as far back as when we were kids playing our favorite games in the backyard...I think you often let me win lol. I hope you never forget that, just like this perfume, it is whats on the inside that's the most valuable thing...what makes you a treasure. I hope you never change, sis, and that you never lose sight of the true meaning of this season—and our lives.

I love you, and always will.

Your brother, Marcus.

P.S.—Sorry if this is a strange gift—it seemed like the right choice at the time. You know, I'm not the best at making decisions but this time I think I did OK. HAHA. I am trying to take steps to change my life...to do the right thing. Dont loose faith! Unfortunatly, that means leaving without saying goodbye. I can only take so much sadness. I'm sorry, but it seems to me that the further I get away from you the less danger you'll be in. Just remember those three special words from when we were kids. That's the key that'll get you through when you find that your stuck. –M

Aria had difficulty reading the last, her vision becoming blurry as she stared at the words. She went to the bathroom to find some tissue then returned to finish the rest. A thought struck her then, that maybe he hadn't yet made it out of town, so she hurried back to the bedroom and got socks and shoes on and then grabbed her coat from where she'd tossed it on a chair the night before. She went to the front door and threw it open.

The snow had finally stopped falling and now she was looking out over a wonderland carpeted in white. There were a set of tracks leading from the front step to the road. No sign of Marcus other than those telltale and ghostly footprints in the snow.

Face it, Aria, she told herself. *He is truly gone.*

She stood on the porch for a while, staring out as if willing him to reappear somehow. The snow had nestled everything in a preternatural silence. There was not a discernible sound other than her own breathing and the creaking of branches from a tree somewhere on the property. Then those sounds of ethereal contentment were joined by one of a manmade nature: The ringtone from her cellphone.

She rushed back to the bedroom, dug through her purse furiously looking for the phone before realizing that she had set it up to charge through the night. She snatched it off the bedside dresser, unplugging it and sliding the bar on the screen to answer it.

"Hello?" She asked. "Marcus?"

"Hey, no...it's...it's Trevor. Just checking in. Is...is everything okay? You sound a bit frantic."

Aria slumped down on the bed. "It's Marcus. I think he's gone."

A moment of silence. "I'm sorry to hear that. I can run out toward the road and see if I can track him down. If he's headed toward the Interstate he might be walking—or hitching a ride. It's a long stretch and there won't be much traffic so I might be able to run him down."

"Can you? I hate to ask for anything else, to be so helpless..."

"I'd be happy to. Let me go and I'll call you when I find him."

If *you find him*, she thought. *I just hope that he's still alive.*

"Thank you so much," she said instead, then hung up.

Numb, she sat on the bed, tried to process everything, the perfume bottle and note clutched in her hand. Finally, she got up and began shoving things into her overnight bag. Since she wasn't planning on trudging through the snow, she quickly realized that she had no way off the property until the good officer Trevor Mason returned for her. She told herself she was just getting herself ready to be able to leave right away when he did return but a part of her knew it was just nervous activity to keep herself from the inevitable conclusion that her brother had either left town or was dead. Either way, another nagging doubt was pressing against her with urgency: That, either way, she might never see him again.

Officer Trevor Mason called again about thirty minutes later. Aria had been sitting on the edge of the bed, gnawing at a fingernail, trying to piece together what her next course of action should be. She considered returning to her home, that running scared like this was something completely foreign to her. Something that Marcus often did...that somehow he'd gotten her to do the night before. At any rate, she needed to do *something.*

When the ringtone began it got only three notes in before she had snatched the phone up and received the call. Trevor was morose, his voice low and apologetic. "Aria...I'm sorry but I saw no sign of him. He's probably caught a lift with a truck driver or something. A lot of people on the road today..."

She knew he had meant it as reassurance but it only brought more frustration. She tried to keep control of her emotions and the desperation of the moment. In a level voice she managed: "Thank you so much. Thanks for checking on it. You've done so much for us, but I'm going to ask you for something else."

"Anything," he said.

"Can you pick me up? I've got to go by the house and..." her voice drifted off as she eyed the perfume bottle. "Well, I got a message from my brother with a gift he left. I think he really is gone, Trevor."

"Okay," he responded. "I'll be back over there to get you as soon as I can. And Aria?"

"Yes?"

"Don't assume the worst. We're going to find your brother and we're going to get down to the nitty-gritty about what is actually going on."

"Thanks. Thank you, Trevor."

They disconnected and Aria sat there for a moment. Then she closed her eyes and prayed that God would keep Marcus safe. By the time she was done, tears had returned to her eyes and she absently wiped them away with the backs of her hands. Remembering work, she dialed Peter Dillahunt and got voicemail. She left a message that she would be in a little late, that a family emergency had come up. Then she hung up and texted him a message with the same basic content. She slipped the phone back into her pocket.

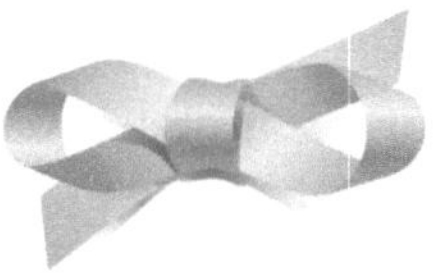

SIX

When Trevor pulled up in the cruiser a while later Aria was standing on the porch waiting for him. He followed her into the kitchen as she sat down at the table and folded her hands together. When she looked up she had tears brimming in her eyes. "I'm not sure exactly what I'm supposed to do next," she said.

"Hey, take it easy for a minute," he said, sliding into the seat opposite her. His voice was soothing, his eyes heavy with concern. She looked at him for a moment and then shook her head. "What's wrong?"

"Marcus," Aria said. "Who knows if anything he's said is even true." She hated herself for voicing her suspicions aloud. To share these thoughts—especially with someone outside of the family—was tantamount to a betrayal. Yet she couldn't help it. The tears broke free, spilling down her cheeks. *How many times have we been through this before with him? How many times has he promised something only to break our trust.*

Trevor scooted closer, taking one of her hands in his own. After a moment, she was able to put aside her shame and face him directly. She detected genuine concern there, which made going on a little easier.

"Drugs have always been a problem for my big brother," she said softly, feeling as if it was more her confession than his. "He used to say that most people would call it a monkey on their back, but that to him it was more akin to a snake coiled around his neck. 'This addiction of mine has teeth,' he once admitted. 'I either fail and it bites me or I try to withstand and I feel suffocated.' He promises he'll quit, even one time said that it was like he was in a car without brakes, speeding toward a brick wall. That he had a wakeup call, knew he was heading for a crash." She shook her head, staring out into the living room but really focusing in on the past. "That was several detoxes ago. After a while, it's really hard to hold out faith in people, even if you love them."

Turning back to him, she said: "Last night, though...man, I thought it might be real for once. I saw something different in his eyes...real fear. But now I'm afraid that he's run off again. Whether it's responsibility or these phantoms that he says are chasing him, he always runs away from it. But he was right: that addiction won't let him go. No matter where he runs it seems to find him. He can escape his family it seems—all the people who care about him, but not the drugs. I just don't know what to do."

Trevor gave her hand a gentle squeeze. "I know this isn't close to being enough, but I want you to know that I'm here. I'll do anything I can to help...you *or* your brother."

"But why?" She asked, new tears springing up. "Why do you care so much? I mean, it's very kind and it does mean a lot. Why would you want to get any more involved in this stuff than you have to?"

"Once upon a time," he said with a smile, "We used to know each other rather well. Do you remember that? I know that we never dated or got romantically involved—whatever you call it in high school. But we were friends...good friends."

"Yeah," Aria said, smiling though tears were falling down her cheeks. "What happened to all that?"

He shrugged, offered a weak smile of his own. "Life. Hesitancy. Who knows? The point is this: I never forgot you, not in all the years that have passed in between then and now. Going the separate directions that life took us, I figured we would never really come back in contact again. At least, not like before. And here you are, flitting back to Anderson's Crossroads like a little bird migrating south for the winter."

She laughed. "Little bird, huh?"

"Sorry," he looked away, a crooked smile on his face. For a moment, watching him, Aria saw in his expression the ghost of the boy that had sent her a rose during the Valentine's Day fundraiser. *What was that? Sixth grade? I would have been in eighth. Not even a kid, we were more like babies. He was always so awkward but that was part of his charm. Innocence and honesty. A girl could do much worse.*

"You've always been so sweet," Aria said. "Even way back then. You've really not changed much, have you? I like that."

He absorbed her words, closing his eyes for a moment as if enjoying a beautiful orchestral piece. When he opened them again he looked directly into her eyes. "Despite the years, I always thought of you from time to time. How could I not? Yeah, life got in the way a little and we had to let God take us in the direction that he wanted for our lives, but it seems like those roads have led back home once more, huh?"

"For now," Aria said, immediately wishing that she could retract them as soon as the words escaped her lips, wishing that she could just buy into a wholesome optimism completely. There had just been too much to bear lately. David's death had been the worst of it, of course, but who knew what the future held? What would happen to Marcus if his demons—either real or fabricated out of a drug-influenced psychosis—couldn't be banished into the darkness once and for all?

"Well," Trevor said, following his own train of thought. "'Now' is all we have control of, isn't it? God holds the future in his hands and we've got this moment. Maybe he'll let us chart a course of our choosing. Maybe it's his will to think about—"

She turned to face him again, her face resolute. *I have to lower my head, bull my way through this,* she thought. *Regardless of whatever old emotions might be fighting to reach the surface.* "I'll fail you," she whispered, her voice hoarse. "My life is a mess...tragedy runs in my family...it's hereditary. Just look at my brother. Me? I'm still trying to get past what happened to my fiancé, David. To process all of it so I can move on. It's not fair to drag someone into this. It's all just such a big mess, Trevor."

"Who said anything about me being dragged into anything?" He asked. "If you haven't noticed, Aria, I'm a big boy now. No one makes me do what I don't wanna do."

"Oh, I've noticed," she chuckled, thankful for the little reprieve from all the weighty thoughts. "You're kind and handsome and...this just...well, it just doesn't seem to be the right time. It might be the 'right now', but it's not right, now. You know? Maybe that'll change. I don't know, there just seems to be so much..."

"That's fine," he said. "I'm not trying to barge in on your life. I just want to help. I want to make sure you're okay. And I want to make sure that whatever it was that your brother was talking about, we get it resolved...either dispelling the fairy tale or uncovering the truth. One way or another, I want to help you get this thing figured out. That's all."

She took a deep breath, let it out. Somehow, the little conversation had helped. Enough at least for her to try and find the logic in what he was saying. Resolved, she nodded her head. "Well, I wish we had something to go on—I mean, about Marcus. He left before we could really delve into what he was even talking about. He left without further explanation...all he left was a Christmas gift and a little note."

Trevor glanced at the bottle. "Perfume? Is that a typical gift siblings would give for one another?"

"Not that I know of," Aria retorted. "Then again, not much about our family is what you'd call 'typical,' per se."

He chuckled. "Might be more representative of the American family than you know. The Mason family isn't exactly something out of 'Leave it to Beaver' either."

"Anyways, it's maybe a little sliver of sunlight. *Hope*, is what I'm saying, I suppose. Marcus has always been the kind to *ask* for stuff: Money, help, food...whatever. Last time I got a birthday or Christmas gift from him we were kids. It's out of character, but that's a good thing. Generosity and thoughtfulness are new concepts as far as my brother is concerned. But...well, I don't know what—if anything—to really take from it."

Trevor considered this, finally reaching forward, and taking the bottle in his hands. "I don't know much about perfume, but it looks..."

"*Expensive?*" She asked. "Well, yeah, it is that. This brand is probably eighty bucks. Hate to think about where he might have gotten the money for it, but it bothers me even more that he did it. Again, these kinds of emotions are not in his general wheelhouse. Wow, I sound like a horrible human being."

Trevor shrugged, smelled the cap. "Smells good."

Aria nodded, half paying attention. "I hate myself for thinking so poorly about my brother. He was just being thoughtful, with it being Christmas and all."

"Maybe," Trevor said. "I mean, sure...but maybe that's not all."

"What do you mean?"

"Well," Trevor began, gently setting the perfume bottle on the table. "Something you said has stuck in my craw. You called it hope. More specifically, a little sliver of sunlight. Maybe there's something in that note that he wrote to try and...well, *illuminate* what's going on. Like some sort of clue—either directly or indirectly—that only you would be able to decipher."

"Sounds like a mystery movie," Aria said. "But okay, I'm game." She reached forward to examine the bottle closer. She read the note to herself again as Trevor waited patiently, saying nothing. Then she re-read it a third time.

"Anything?" He asked.

"Well, there is one very overt part that I didn't take for a clue at first, but more of a *secret*. For the two of us, not in regard to whoever it is that is supposedly chasing him." She opened the note up again. "This part: '*Just remember those three special words from when we were kids. That's the key that'll get you through when you're stuck.*'"

Trevor sat suddenly upright. "That's not a clue, that's a punch in the nose. What special words when you were kids is he talking about?"

Aria stared off into the middle distance, remembering. "Something he'd always say when we were kids and we were doing some secret project that only we knew about: Building a treehouse, starting a private little club, the time he caught a frog and we tried to sneak it inside and let it live out its admittedly short life in the upstairs bathtub. He'd say: 'Only for us, sis, okay? This part is only for us.' Sibling secrets. Before you get close friends and girlfriends or boyfriends you have your sibling and you're super tight...at least we were. Those are the three words I suppose: Only. For. Us. But I'm not sure really what to do with that little tidbit of information."

Trevor mulled this over himself. Then, after a moment he let out a pent-up breath and said: "I don't want to nose into your business, but do you mind if I read the note?"

"Sure," Aria said, readily handing the bottle with the note attached to him. "Maybe you can come up with something."

He spent five minutes frowning down at the note then staring at the ceiling while he tried to uncover the secret...if there even was one. Then he gently set the perfume down on the table and stared at it as if it was a small pet that might turn and bite him at any moment.

"Well, super sleuth," Aria joked. "Come up with anything?"

"Uh...no, nothing. Pardon the pun but I haven't got a clue."

Aria shrugged. "Then we'll let it marinate. Maybe later we'll have some kind of

ingenious breakthrough and decipher the riddle."

"For his sake at least, I hope we do."

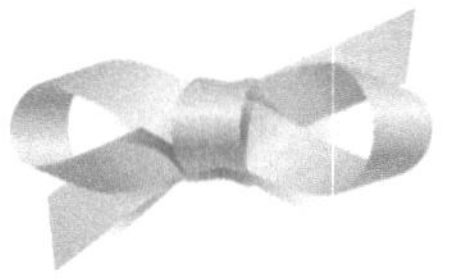

SEVEN

As the morning bled into the afternoon the ominous dread seemed to melt away from the day, helped along in no short measure by the spirit of the season. Dripping icicles reflected the sun like spikes of silver, and the vast expanse of snow stretching into the distance seemed so stark a contrast to thoughts of danger.

Aria had mentioned to Trevor needing to make one last appearance at Peter Dillahunt's veterinary clinic before Christmas, and as they drove through snow-covered field after field, she could feel the normalcy begin to settle over her once more. She was still bothered by her brother's sudden exit from Anderson's Corners but she had to remind herself that his sudden disappearances weren't really anything new.

She had detached the note from the perfume, folded it once, and now carried it in her pocket. She wanted it close, a reminder of him. She seemed to extract joy from the message like a honeybee would extract nectar from a honeysuckle. At the same time, it was a painful reminder of what they'd lost throughout the years.

Trevor volunteered to drive her to the vet's office, promising to pick her back up when she was done. Aria thanked him profusely then watched as he drove away. When the vehicle was gone she turned, entered through the glass door of DILLAHUNT VETERINARIAN CLINIC, and saw the good Dr. Dillahunt frantically gathering up his hat and a tweed coat. "What's going on?" Aria asked as she walked into the shop.

"Ah, you're just in time my dear," he said breathlessly. "You ready to assist with a delivery?"

"You're doing Christmas deliveries? Why do..." Aria caught herself, feeling foolish as she finally deciphered the reason for his rushed and anxious deportment. "Oh! *That* kind of a delivery."

He chuckled. "Yep. The Jacksons called a few moments ago. Their mare is about to give birth. We gotta hurry if we want to get there in time."

Dillahunt didn't need to say anything more than that. Aria turned, going right back out the door as she followed him outside. She jumped into the passenger seat of his truck and they accelerated away from the property, turning onto the freshly plowed blacktop of CR-25 a minute later. Cautious about any black ice that might be lingering, Dillahunt kept the needle pegged at 55 but didn't dare push it any faster. It was twelve miles into the country before they'd reach the Jackson farm.

Like he was breaking out of trance he looked at her with concern and asked: "Is there something wrong with your car?"

"No..." Aria looked out the window, frantically trying to gather her thoughts. She didn't really want to go into the circumstances surrounding her brother's unexpected visit the night before. Not right then, at least. "Felt safer with a ride out here, and Officer Mason was nice enough to oblige."

He shot her a sideways glance, the corners of his mouth pulled up just slightly enough to form the hint of a knowing smile. "Okay." Then, a few moments later: "He's a good guy, that Officer Mason."

She let it hang in the air but she was still turned away, feeling the flush rising in her cheeks. She didn't want to go into *that* either.

They rode along in silence for a while. Aria was familiar with Winston and Tamara Jackson, though she did not know them particularly well. A couple in their late seventies, Winston still tirelessly toiled on the family farm as he had for the past fifty years. Farm folk were a particularly hearty bunch, Aria knew, since her parents also had a smaller farm when she was younger. It was nothing for them to put in eighty hours of work or more a week. This she knew was true of Winston Jackson, who not only farmed but had a job at the mill as well. That was another thing about farmers: They always had to have a backup plan in case the weather and the harvest didn't cooperate. Hard work and heartache, that seemed to be the farmer's lot.

There was nothing more beautiful to Aria than a clear blue sky above fields of pristine white. Here and there it even shone blue. The only downside was that the snow was already beginning to melt away. Aria could imagine the kids in town dragging their sleds over to the little hill behind the town square, trying to make a roller coaster ride out of the mush. Even a sluggish ride could be remedied by the shared excitement of one's peers. At the very least, the snow was in good shape to supply an endless armament of soft cannon balls. Cold and wet, the young soldiers would shuffle home eventually to huddle over hot mugs of cocoa and maybe even a Christmas cookie or two as they strategized about their next campaign.

She smiled to herself as she gazed out the window, realizing that those days weren't all that far in the past. Dillahunt busily fiddled with the dial of the radio as he tried to coax out a clear signal for the local country station. He finally found it, the festive sounds of *Do you hear what I hear?* floating from the speakers.

Aria smiled to herself. Thoughts of Christmases of her youth was exactly what she needed right then in order to try and forget about the frenzy of the previous night. All those years of missed connections with her brother and the overshadowing sorrow of a relationship that had never really coalesced to much more than the proverbial ships passing in the night. His past always seemed to overtake him, to disrupt whatever pure motives and good intentions he'd tried to follow through on. She could even begin to believe that everything her brother had been worried about was merely paranoid delusions. She whispered a prayer for him, that he would find his way out of the darkness of addiction and into the light. It was a prayer similar to hundreds she'd uttered before.

The Jackson farm was a sprawling complex enclosed by a white picket fence and an arching entrance with the family crest centered above. The long, winding drive led to a beautiful two-story farmhouse nestled between a scattering of towering pines. Behind the house was the barn, a massive construction that housed a half dozen horses and farm equipment. Lying dormant, the broad expanse of the acreage, bristling with healthy green corn stalks in the spring was now just a featureless wasteland waiting for more promising climes. A sullen empire of white.

Tamara Jackson scurried out onto the porch to meet them as they pulled up to the farmhouse. She greeted Peter Dillahunt and Aria and gestured toward the barn. "Winston is already there," she said, leading the way on foot.

Dillahunt guided the pickup truck to the barn and then he and Aria hopped out. The sounds of the old mare whinnying floated on the crisp air. Dillahunt grabbed a satchel from the bed of the truck and strolled with Aria into the barn.

Winston Jackson caught them approaching in his peripheral and turned to greet them as they reached the stall in which he was crouched over the struggling mare. "Ah! Y'all made it!" He said good-naturedly as Dillahunt let himself into the stall and held the door open for Aria to follow. "She's foaling."

Dillahunt scooted across the hay-strewn floor, crouching down and speaking to the horse in a soothing voice. Gently, he placed one palm on her muzzle and stroked it softly. "All right, mama," he said, "let's see what we can do about helping get your young 'un into this world, huh?"

The mare snorted, her eyes wide in distress.

"How long has she been contracting?" Dillahunt asked quietly.

"At least an hour now," Winston said. "Far as I can tell."

The mare shifted and there was a sudden rupturing of fluids flooding out over the fresh straw. "Here we go," Dillahunt said. The mare craned her neck as if surprised by her body's response, a leg kicking at the air. "Easy does it, darlin.'"

Aria watched closely as the foal's legs appeared, the hooves sliding out from its mother. This was her favorite part of vet work, and the process of animal childbirth never ceased to fascinate her. As its legs appeared, the foal was trying to wriggle its way out. Most of the time their job as vets was to monitor and assist when it became necessary: When there was some kind of medical emergency that required special intervention, they'd move in and take a much more active role. So far, this delivery was going along as well as could be expected.

The foal continued to work its way out of the translucent womb, finally emerging as a healthy foal.

"Mom and baby seem to be just fine," Dillahunt observed. "Now we need to let them rest and stay warm."

"I've got a blanket here," Winston Jackson said.

"Shouldn't need it," Dillahunt said, observing the foal and its mother. "It's plenty warm in here."

They stayed for a while longer, observing the mother and foal and making sure there weren't any problems. Afterwards, Winston lead them out of the barn and up to the house where they were promised fresh coffee. "Thank you for getting here so quickly," Tamara said.

"No problem at all," Dillahunt said. "And thanks for the coffee!"

Once they were finished and exiting the Jackson home, Aria asked the vet if she could get a lift into town. Dillahunt graciously agreed—and without any sly remarks about the good police officer this time. She was feeling much better, her cares all but forgotten, like a cloud dissipating to give way to a sun-drenched day. They drove back to Anderson's Crossroads and Aria had him drop her off at the diner, promising to be at work bright and early on the 26th.

She perused a menu. It was still early enough for breakfast so she ordered a couple eggs over medium, bacon, hash browns, and toast. The waitress set a steaming mug of coffee in front of her as well. She had just taken her first sip when she sensed someone nearby.

"Mind if I join you?" Officer Trevor Mason asked.

She smiled. "Please do."

He slid into the booth opposite her and set his hat gently on the table. When the waitress appeared a few moments later he ordered a cup of coffee. The waitress flitted off and Trevor turned his attention back to Aria. "So...how was your morning?"

Aria recounted the delivery of the foal and her overall feeling of renewed optimism that had come with the new day. "I'm hoping that Marcus caught a bus and is either going to Arizona to see my family for the holidays or that at least he has somewhere else in mind that he can go where there are friends nearby. *Good* friends, I should add."

"Yeah, let's hope that's true. I'd hate for him to be by himself for the holidays." He looked at her a little closer, cocking his head as the corners of his lips turned up in a ghost of a smile. "How are you doing though? Really?"

Aria started to answer then stopped herself, taking a breath. She gazed out the window at the cars puttering down the street, the scattering of passersby walking briskly between destinations, hands plunged into the pockets of their coats and pants. When she turned back she had a smile of her own. "Honestly, I'm doing much better."

"That's great to hear."

"Have you had a busy morning?" She asked him.

He snorted. "Here...in *this* sleepy little town? You know that rarely does *anything* ever happen in Anderson's Crossroads. I guess I should be happy about that."

"Indeed. I guess police business is one of the truly rare vocations in which the less that happens the better, huh?"

"Right." He smiled, then folded his hands together and leaned forward. "So...today is December 23rd, which means that Christmas is day after tomorrow. Got any big plans?"

"Not particularly. Now that my family is spread out we don't do a whole lot for Christmas, at least not together. However, my church family is having a special candlelight service on Christmas Eve if you'd like to join me."

"Oh?"

"Yeah," Aria said. "We do it every year. Why don't you come?"

He leaned back, grinning. "Are you asking me on a date? For real?"

She laughed. "It doesn't have to be that serious...but yeah, I guess I am."

He shook his head. "I thought this day would never come."

She swatted at him. "Grow up."

He laughed. "Yes...I would be honored to be able to join you. Thank you."

"Don't thank me yet," Aria quipped. "I might be an awful date...you never know."

"Good point." He took a sip of his coffee, then set it down with his hands wrapped around the mug as if to draw warmth from it. "Anything else happen that might raise concerns about the whole mess last night?"

Aria considered this. "No...I had a restful night. Thank you for watching over us. I really do mean that."

"You're welcome."

Aria's breakfast arrived a few minutes later and she prayed before digging in. Trevor sipped his coffee, and they chatted a little but he was soon glancing at his watch. "Guess I better get back to work."

"Okay," Aria said. "So... I'll see you tomorrow night?"

"I'll pick you up," Trevor said. "If that's all right with you, I mean."

"Sounds perfect. The service starts at seven, so...six thirty?"

He snatched his hat off the table. "Six thirty it is."

The bell over the door rang as Trevor exited. Aria watched him make his way to his cruiser and open the door. Before he slid in he glanced at her, giving a little wave of his hand and a warm smile.

Aria felt a little flutter in her stomach and then shook her head. These schoolgirl crushes seemed a little silly. *But boy can I get used to that smile,* she thought.

The air was crisp with very little wind, the sky a bright, deep blue. Aria decided to grab a few things from town before returning home. Then she strolled along the sidewalk—the snow-covered wonderland now just a memory, the walks having been scraped clean and now dusted with salt, the streets plowed. People were bustling about, trying to finish their last-minute Christmas shopping. Christmas music was playing from unseen outdoor speakers in an effort to encourage a festive, upbeat, and overspending mood. Currently, Bing

Crosby was crooning about Christmas cards and longing for another white Christmas.

She crossed the street, slipped into an alley, and emerged onto her street. A quarter mile later she was walking up her own front path—this one, unfortunately, not freshly swept—and onto the porch. She fished out her keys and was in the process of selecting the right one when she was struck by the unsettling realization that she wouldn't need it. Someone had already visited, having busted through the broken door and slipped inside.

EIGHT

Feeling a numbness deep in her bones, as if observing the whole thing outside of herself, Aria remained on the porch, staring at the broken doorframe. Less afraid than angry now, she fought to retain her composure. There it was, the frame splintered, the deadbolt still engaged as it had stubbornly hung on even while the rest of the door tore through the housing, stark evidence that her brother's fears were not the ramblings of a mind possessed by an unrealistic paranoia. That her refusal to believe what he had been saying was a betrayal of the worst kind. That he had left not just because he felt that he was in danger, but that he truly *was* in danger. That he did it—at least in part—so that he could protect her, the sister who hadn't even believed him.

She felt tears welling up in her eyes but she pushed them away. *Not now.* She didn't deserve to feel sad right now. Her brother was miles away, somewhere alone and...and...who knew what else? Whatever he had been involved in had been all too real, had followed him to Anderson's Crossroads. Aria's life was in jeopardy, as was anyone else's whom she interacted with. *Whoever these people are, they know where you live!*

It was almost as if that frantic inner voice had been spoken aloud, just over her shoulder. Aria turned around, certain that she'd see someone waiting there for her, gun in hand. About to end it all. Instead, there was just the silent, snow-covered ground. Then she thought about something else and stepped forward to examine the ground itself. There was a single set of footprints coming up the walk—the ones she had just left moments ago. But to her left, coming alongside the porch was another set of footprints. She tried to put the timetable of the previous evening together in her mind, and eventually arrived at the conclusion that these footprints had been left at some point after she and Officer Trevor Mason had arrived. *Was a stranger watching as we were inside? Did they follow us afterward?* Then the worst thought of them all: *Do they know that I stayed overnight at Trevor's great grandmother's home?*

She knew that she needed to call Trevor, and decided that, in time, she would. First, she wanted to take a look inside.

Easing the door open the rest of the way, the interior of the house gave up its secrets. Gasping, Aria hesitated at the threshold, a trembling hand drifting to her mouth as if to contain the next sounds that might involuntarily escape.

Emotions rose within her: Anger, and fear, and anguish. The sense of being utterly and completely violated. The loss of all that lent a feeling of security and innocence. Someone had broken into her home—her sanctuary—but they had ransacked it as well. This last injustice caused something to break inside of her and now the tears were escaping in a sudden flood. She looked through blurred vision at the fallout. There was debris everywhere: Smashed pictures, papers flung about, furniture overturned. Whoever had been here had been quite thorough, even in their carelessness. *They were looking for something. Whatever Marcus had that he wanted to keep hidden, they're looking for it.*

She stepped inside, swinging the door closed behind her but then being reminded of the fact that it wouldn't latch because someone had destroyed the locking mechanism. Standing in the living room, she absorbed the devastation, the lone survivor of a bombing strafe standing in the ruins. It was like a tornado had erupted within the house but had also been contained there as well. *What were they looking for?* She wondered. *And why hadn't Marcus just gone to the authorities in the first place?*

The answer to that first question remained a mystery, but she figured that she could guess about the second. Her brother had had so many run-ins with the authorities—none of them the type that could be described as 'cordial'—and it was no wonder that he didn't consider the police to be potential allies, even in as extreme a situation as this. He simply didn't trust them. That was part of the problem, but the greater problem was one Aria was still trying her best to ignore...one she didn't want to accept.

Whatever evidence he has against this shadowy group of people may very well implicate him as well. Perhaps he thought of it less as evidence and more as an insurance policy.

Aria certainly didn't like thinking along those lines.

Forcing herself to take a step forward, she oriented herself toward the kitchen and numbly began moving in that direction, stepping over broken keepsakes and the other debris scattered on the ground. She hesitated, bracing herself, then stepped inside the room.

Drawers had been yanked open and riffled through. The pantry closet door was open as well, boxes overturned and their contents dumped on the ground. Aria kneeled down and righted some of the open containers, her anger growing fiercer as she examined the sugar, salt, and other powders that had been scattered across the floor.

She went room to room this way, each revelation a new injustice that drove her closer to the edge of fury. She saw all of these things through a veil of unshed tears. Her couch had been slashed horizontally like the belly of some smooth-skinned beast; The TV had been ripped from the wall and tossed carelessly aside, the cabinet overturned and spilling DVDs across the carpet; Mail, coupons, circulars, and other paperwork was carelessly flung across the room; Closet doors stood open, some smashed, all the contents from the shelves haphazardly and thoughtlessly dumped. *How could you do this?* She wondered, then wasn't sure if she was talking to the faceless phantoms that had invaded her privacy or her brother Marcus, who had brought all of this to her doorstep.

She grabbed a fire poker—just in case any of the bandits was still there—and trudged up the stairs. The second floor revealed a similar scene of carnage. She didn't want to see any more but was helpless but to keep going, visiting each and every room, not knowing how much more she could handle but at the same time just wanting to get it over with.

Another thought had intruded on her mind, a possibility she resisted but finally entertained: *What if Marcus did this? What if he tore the house apart looking for money?* She knew she shouldn't follow the direction those thoughts would lead her, but she was not immune from the suspicion. Of everything, it did make sense, didn't it? The whole paranoia about being followed could have been the result of drug use or simply a cover for what he'd do later. Maybe he hadn't left town at all, just came back here looking for cash or something he could sell.

Stop! Don't think that way, just...just don't. She turned around, her teeth gritted and tears still falling, and made her way back downstairs.

This can't be happening. Not here...not to me. This has to be some kind of strange dream. No...a nightmare. I'll soon wake up in my bed and all this will have been a dream best forgotten.

Of course, that kind of thinking was just a fantasy; this was all too real. She didn't need to pinch herself to know that. She felt helpless, impotent in her rage. All around her was the evidence of unknown men having broken into her home—her life—and destroyed almost everything she had ever owned...the accumulations of a lifetime to which were attached her fondest memories. Worse, they had robbed her of any sense of security. A sobering reminder that, even in a small town like Anderson's Crossroads you are never immune to such devastation. She feared that she would never feel truly safe again.

And there, in the midst of the carnage, a truth that cut through her emotions like a knife: *Marcus wouldn't have done this. He wouldn't have destroyed everything like this, even if he was desperate. I refuse to believe that because if he did then this man who is my brother is someone I've never really known before. I can't accept that possibility.*

Somehow, that made her feel a little better. She knew in her heart she was right. She wasn't sure if Marcus would steal from her but she was positive that he wouldn't do this.

Returning to the living room, she sat down on the ruined couch and stared at the damage. *Why, God? Why did this have to happen? What has Marcus gotten himself involved in?* She absently wiped away fresh tears, blinking. She remained there for a moment, processing everything. Then, after suffering through a suitable process of dejection, she attempted to realign herself, to refocus both on her physical surroundings as well as the implications of what had happened. She felt herself softening toward her brother. *Only for us.* Could she share the bad along with the good? If her brother was really in trouble, shouldn't she do all she could to help him? *Of course!*

Plucking her cellphone out of her purse, she dialed Trevor. A moment later he picked up and she took a few minutes to explain what had happened. The concern for her wellbeing was evident in his voice and he said he'd be there as soon as possible. She thanked him and hung up.

She thought of her childhood, how Marcus had been an inseparable part of just about every childhood memory. They had grown up together but somehow they'd since grown apart. She wondered what had taken him down that brambly path to drug use. She ached for him afresh, whispered another tear-filled prayer that he would be safe. That he'd be made *whole*. That this whole mess would be resolved somehow. How much of her life had been spent with him, shared with him, influenced by her big brother? *Only for us* had marked countless magical discoveries and unforgettable adventures. It was like the password for an exclusive clubhouse.

Reminded of the note, she carefully pulled the perfume bottle out of her travel bag and looked over it again. It was written in his typical scrawl, but appeared as if he might have taken a little more care this time in writing this message to her. She was suddenly very happy that this gift hadn't been destroyed...that she'd kept it with her all along.

She blinked, then looked down at it again. Perhaps that was the point. *Marcus picked out this gift to tell you how thoughtful he was being. Isn't that what was so unique about it? As strange as it might be to purchase perfume for a sister, it was even stranger that Marcus thought to buy anything at all. So strange as to be...what? Certainly, out of the realm of the coincidental. But could it be evidence of something more? Something of great importance?*

She turned the bottle over in her hands, examining it like an archaeologist that had uncovered some rare and valuable relic. Perfume was a gift most women would enjoy receiving, but even more than that it was a gift that a man would have no use for...even men of a certain deplorable bent.

That's it, Aria! He wanted to pass along to you what these men were after! It's not about the gift as much as it is about the note attached! Whoever did this wouldn't think of perfume as being any more than that, a woman's gift, certainly nothing that would hold any kind of intrinsic value to them. What if this note is the very thing they were looking for? What if it was written in order to communicate some hidden secret...one only you would be able to decipher?

She re-read the note, this time with much more urgency. Instead of just being a nice sentiment from a brother from whom she'd grown distant, she read the message this time with the intent of looking for some underlying message.

Little Sis—

I hope you have a Merry Christmas. It was so good to see you again, even under these circumstances. You are such a buietiful person—I knew this even when long ago, when we were kids playing our favorite games in the backyard...I think you often let me win lol. I hope you never forget that, just like this perfume, it is whats on the inside that's the most valuable thing...what makes you a treasure. I hope you never change, sis, and that you never lose sight of the true meaning of this season—and our lives.

I love you, and always will.

Your brother, Marcus.

P.S.—Sorry if this is a strange gift—it seemed like the right choice at the time. You know, I'm not the best at making decisions but this time I think I did OK. HAHA. I am trying to take steps to change my life...to do the right thing. Dont loose faith! Unfortunatly, that means leaving without saying goodbye. I can only take so much sadness. I'm sorry, but it seems to me that the further I get away from you the less danger you'll be in. Just remember those three special words from when we were kids. That's the key that'll get you through when you find that your stuck. –M

A certain phrase stuck out to her this time:

Just like this perfume, it is what is on the inside that is the most valuable thing...what makes you a treasure.

She examined the perfume, handling it carefully like it was some kind of artifact.

The words "valuable" and "treasure" stuck out in her mind, but she couldn't see anything special about it. She removed the cap and sniffed at the atomizer. *Smells like perfume,* she thought to herself. Cap still in hand, she turned the bottle over, examining the bottom but finding nothing out of the ordinary. Then she studied the cap itself and froze a moment later.

What do we have here?

At first she thought it was some sort of anti-theft device fixed to the inside of the cap but as she worked her fingers in there and finally got it dislodged she realized it was something else. About an inch in length and half that in diameter, the item was red and black and instantly recognizable when she slid the little lever forward and a silver nub appeared.

A flash drive.

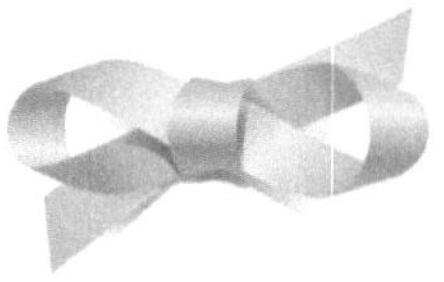

NINE

They sat side by side on the couch, Trevor turning the flash drive over and over in his hand. "So...this is what they were after. I wonder what valuable secrets this thing might have stored inside. I suppose that it could be anything."

"One way to find out," Aria said, standing. "I think these scumbags stole my laptop but right now I think I'd feel a little safer in public anyways. There's computers and WiFi at the library."

Trevor stood. "Then what are we waiting for?"

She rode with him in the squad car to the library. The parking lot was half full, and they found a slot near the front of the lot. They walked up to the front door. Holiday hours were posted on the front door and Aria checked her watch. "The sign says that they're closed tomorrow but they'll be open today until 4. We've got plenty of time."

Aria had detached her brother's note from the perfume bottle and put it in her purse. Once they were settled in one of the stations with the desktop computer firing up, she withdrew it and spread it out on the table between them. "I feel like the worst sister in the world," she said. "He was telling the truth the whole time, and I didn't believe a word he said. Now he's gone."

"Well, we got the message and that's the important thing," Trevor said. "Let's hope that what we find on this flash drive will not only exonerate your brother but can lead us to the arrest of whoever is behind all of this."

"Agreed."

The computer seemed to be doing a lot of furious whirring and humming but not getting them anywhere. Aria tapped her foot impatiently under the table while Trevor leaned forward, staring with a look of intense anticipation at the screen. Finally, the webpage for the library popped up and Aria was able to punch in a few details to get access to the web. But going online wasn't what they were primarily interested in...not yet at least. She fumbled with the flash drive and finally slid it into the port. A moment later a security window popped up, the icon flashing on a little box that said PASSWORD. Like a tapping foot, the blinking cursor patiently waited for her to supply the missing credentials.

She stared at it for a moment before turning to Trevor. "Don't ask me," he said. "I don't have a clue what the password would be nor am I much of a hacker."

A message below the blinking cursor informed them that they would have three cracks at it before being locked out for a twenty-four-hour period. In smaller type, the message read that one number, and one capital letter was a necessary part of the code.

"This is not good," she said.

"Does he have a favorite sports team?"

"I guess. But which one? He's a fan of the University of Nebraska but as far as professional teams are concerned he follows mainly the Kansas City teams. The Chiefs won in 2023 and '24—that'd be a good bet."

Aria shrugged. She then typed in CHIEFS24 and pressed enter. The computer issued a note that sounded far from positive, and the password was summarily rejected.

"Well, that's one down and two to g—"

Trevor suddenly clamped a hand onto the back of her arm. Stunned, she shot a glance at him but he was looking toward the front of the library. "What?" She asked, trying to follow the direction of his gaze. "What is it?"

He lifted an index finger, pressed it against his lips. "It looks like we've got some out-of-towners visiting for the holidays," he muttered in a hushed tone.

Aria found the pair that Trevor had noticed: A large bald man in a grey trench coat and a slim tall dude dressed in jeans and a black jacket, his eyes sharp and weasel like. They were looking around the library, and they stood out like men in swim trunks at a hockey game.

"Let's get rolling before Laurel and Hardy spot us," Trevor suggested. "Grab the flash drive."

Aria nodded; her eyes fixed on the men. She reached out, ejected the flash drive and slipped it into a pocket. Then she backed her way out of the internet, closing windows until the library's main screen appeared again. Finally, for good measure, she shut the computer down.

Ducking down behind the monitor, Trevor nodded to their left. Aria returned the nod and together they stood. Just in time for the weaselly one to look directly at them.

"Move!" Aria said urgently, her eyes wide as the pair at the front of the library made a dash toward them.

Trevor led the way, slipping in between the bookshelves before breaking into a run. Aria tried to keep up, her head lowered as she rushed past the spines of reference books. She could see the window just beyond them, offering a tantalizing prospect of freedom. In her mind, Aria tried to figure out the possible escape routes, though she already knew that going through the front doors—the ones through which the two thugs had entered—would be the most advantageous choice.

Trevor seemed to realize that as well because when he reached the other side of the building he turned to the right. Bolting forward, he narrowly missed a high school girl emerging from between the stacks, a pile of books in her arms and her glasses sitting crookedly on her nose. "Excuse me, sir," she protested, turning in time for him to brush by without an all-out collision.

Aria followed, muttering an apology of her own. She glanced through the stacks as they passed, searching for any sign of the bad guys. She was thinking they were out in front of them when the slim one appeared behind them, emerging from the stacks about twenty feet away. The worse news was that he had a pistol in his hand.

"Trevor!" She cried, grabbing hold of him by the back of his jacket. He half-turned, looking first at her alarmed expression and then past her at the man with the gun. She pulled him to the right and they dove in between the shelves as the slim man aimed for them.

"Go!" She said. "He has a gun!"

"Yeah," Trevor panted. "I saw! I have one, too, but this is no place for a shoot-out...not if I can help it."

They started down the aisles at a full sprint. Aria wondered where the more rotund of the pair might be. *Hardy, I suppose you could say. That one back there with the gun is Laurel.*

Just then Laurel appeared, aiming the gun at them again. Without thinking, Aria stopped, spinning around, and grabbed hold of the shelves. She yanked down on it—hard, like a contestant at the big wheel on *The Price is Right*—and the books started tumbling toward the ground, the shelves following in a crash. At the same time there was a thunderous gunshot, immediately followed by terrified screams.

Aria did not wait to see what would happen next because she was starting forward again, the calamity of tumbling books and gunmen left behind.

They reached the main aisle and rushed across.

People were darting through the library like startled deer in a meadow, dodging this way and that, some making a quick flight toward the entrance. Others were crouching in fright behind desks and other obstacles, hoping that they wouldn't be discovered. Hiding was not something that she or Trevor could afford to do...the gunmen were out for the kill and they were the targets.

Aria shot a glance to her right and saw the larger man—Hardy—wading toward them through the crowd. He also had a gun in his hand and a very uncharitable look on his flushed face. They kept going forward, the little alcove housing the restrooms and a drinking fountain fast approaching. From previous visits, Aria knew that there was a staircase dead ahead. At least they seemed to be moving in the right direction.

Reaching the alcove, Trevor paused, just enough of a hesitation for her to less graciously barrel by him and slam against the push bar. Grabbing the handrail, she started down. She could hear Trevor's footsteps coming right behind her.

Aria remembered an occasion of sitting around with friends and lamenting the poor screenwriting that often occurred in horror movies in which either the lone hero or future victim would choose to go *upstairs* instead of down and outside. Perhaps that idea was playing in her head when she came through the door and decided on heading *down* the stairs. Without any time to protest, Trevor followed right on her heels and only when they'd reached the bottom did they realize that the next floor down was marked *BASEMENT and* might just as have put them in an even worse position than going to a higher floor. Like mice trapped in a corner by a cat. Or characters trapped trying to escape a worn trope.

There was no time for regrets. Aria turned the knob, opening the door on a darkened room. Fumbling for the light switch, she finally found it and flipped it on. At that moment they heard the door slam from above, frantic but indistinguishable voices floating down. Aria grabbed Trevor's hand and she pulled him further into the room, the door latching behind them of its own accord.

The place was filled with four-drawer filing cabinets, the kind that held ancient records and dusty files. For now, they functioned to provide a little cover and that was the important thing. Aria and Trevor disappeared into the catacombs of metal cabinets, hunched over so that they would be out of view once Laurel and Hardy arrived.

And the other men did arrive in short order, barging through the door less than thirty seconds after Aria and Trevor had made their way into the room. At the sound of their visitor's arrival, Aria and Trevor grew very quiet, carefully measuring each step so as to not give themselves away.

Aria had never been down here before, and now she was starting to feel the unsettling weight of her impulsive decision, the tightness of the quarters. Lining one side of the room were narrow windows—five in all—perhaps four foot by two, eight feet off the ground. Other than that, it was apparent there would be no other avenue of escape than the door they'd all just came through, and it was certain that the thugs would not just let them waltz out of there. *Great job, Aria. You trapped both Trevor and yourself down here. What're you going to do now?*

She didn't immediately have an answer for that one. The best she could do as far as a plan of action was concerned was to simply survive. She also reminded herself that Trevor was armed. At least they weren't going down without a fight.

Trevor didn't look like he was of a mind to just surrender, either. He put a finger to his lips and then motioned with the same finger away from where they stood. Aria nodded, as if to say, *Lead the way, Sir Trevor.*

He shimmied around one end of the filing cabinets before raising the gun and peering over the top. Suddenly, his voice boomed out: "This is Officer Trevor Mason of the Anderson's Crossroads Police. Put your guns down and raise your hands. It's over and I'm bringing both of you in. Dead or alive, that's your choice."

There followed a short barking laugh, though Aria couldn't have said if it was the taller or shorter one who was the culprit. But then a gravelly voice called out: "There's two of us...how 'bout you put *your* gun down?"

Aria remained still, watching Trevor. He was listening carefully, trying to pinpoint where the voice had come from.

One thing that the bad guy said rang true, though: Two guns were better than one. They were at a distinct disadvantage.

Trevor shifted forward, crossing to the next filing cabinet, where he hunkered down, listening. Waiting patiently for the others to make the next move. As it turned out he didn't have to wait too long before there came the squeak of a shoe across the tile. Trevor bolted forward, as quick and as fast as a rabbit in a meadow, the gun in one hand. He disappeared around the corner.

Where is he going? Aria wondered. *He's left me here all alone!*

Distantly, a sound came to them: Police sirens were echoing along the buildings outside. *That should make them a little restless,* she thought. *The teams might not be even right now but in another couple minutes they will be.*

She heard movement then, originating from a few feet from behind her. She jerked her head around, saw nothing there. Then, coming from the other end of the room, she heard a violent screech of metal and one of them men cried out. Aria took the opportunity to scoot down her aisle, her heart thumping in her chest.

There was another collision of body against metal and then she saw a flash as the smaller, rotund man—the one they'd dubbed Hardy—moved across the aisle in front of Aria, not noticing her huddled there. She had the slimmest of glimpses of his passage, enough to see the black shape of a gun in his hand.

"Gotcha!" The man said. "Don't move a muscle or I won't hesitate to shoot you right here and now!"

Aria shifted forward slowly, duckwalking toward the door to the room.

"Drop your gun!" The man shouted.

Aria peeked around the corner, saw Hardy standing there looming over Trevor, who had apparently taken a fall in the scuffle with the thin man—Laurel—who was nowhere in sight.

"Okay, okay," Trevor said, dangling the gun out in his hand like a cat offering a dead mouse to his master. "Take it easy now...don't make anything worse than it has to be."

"Oh, we're *way* past that now," Hardy scoffed, snorting laughter. "You two—and that loser Marcus—you've done more than enough damage already. We're the clean-up crew."

"Just don't shoot. Just take it easy." Trevor gazed up at him. The man, who had appeared to be much smaller a few minutes ago, now loomed over him, a giant with a gun pointed straight at his head, the barrel looking as large as a cannon's.

"Where is the flash drive?" The man demanded. Trevor paused and so Hardy pushed the gun closer, the muzzle now bare inches from Trevor's forehead. "Where is it? Tell me now or in the next couple seconds you're going to have your skull rearranged."

"I don't have it," Trevor pleaded. "I swear, I don't—"

"Shut up!" Hardy pointed the gun at him angrily, his finger against the trigger. His eyes were wide, his face flushing beet-red, and the first trickles of sweat snaking down his forehead and into his eyes. "You've got 'til three then I blow you into another dimension. Got it? *One!*"

"Look, man," Trevor said. "The girl's got it and by now she's long gone, slipped out in the fracas a second ago, I—"

"*Two!*"

"Look, it's too late. The other officers are on their way and you won't help your position at all if you kill a cop. Listen..."

Hardy's lips pursed, his tongue squeezing between his teeth to say that final number when something red flashed through the air. Trevor's eyes widened as Aria's face came into view, the red item in her hand heavy and solid and blurring through the air.

It slammed into the side of Hardy's head and he crumpled to the floor. Only then did Trevor see what weapon Aria had used to knock him out: a fire extinguisher.

She stood over Hardy, who lie motionless on the ground.

"Did I...did I kill him?" Aria asked worriedly, dropping the extinguisher on the ground where it landed with a loud but hollow clang.

"He'll have a little bit of a headache," Trevor observed, "but I think he'll be okay. Unfortunately."

"Thing was heavy," Aria said, rubbing a shoulder.

"Don't feel bad, though," Trevor said. "I basically did the same to his friend."

Aria looked past Hardy to Laurel, who was half hidden in shadows the next aisle over. Like his partner, Laurel was out of commission, lying on his back with his mouth gaping open as if taking a midafternoon siesta.

The sirens were building. The cops were about to pull up.

"Okay," Trevor said. "Let's get the police down here to finish this up."

TEN

They drove together in silence to the police station. Trevor had spent the last twenty minutes on the phone, filling the chief in on what had happened—at least as much as they could make sense of it—and were duly told to give him the rest of the details in person. Chief Mike Stowell didn't exactly blame them for all of it but he wasn't exactly happy, either.

The two thugs were taken (by police escort) to the hospital the next town over, both with nasty bumps on their head and much of the fight taken out of them. Chief Stowell informed Trevor of the fact that an FBI team out of Omaha was enroute. That gave them a little precious time to try and unpuzzle what evidence they did have before they had to turn it over to the feds. Trevor figured Chief Stowell was thinking along those same lines.

Once they arrived at the station they were seated in the large room usually reserved for meetings and morning roll call. Chief Stowell was in one of the seats that the lower ranking officers usually occupied, leaning forward with his arms on his knees and his face twisted up into what was either confusion or—at the very least—deep concern. It wasn't every day that domestic terrorists (as he was keen on calling them) descended upon your small town in the middle of Nebraska. In the meanwhile, Aria had commandeered a laptop from the station and now the contents of the flash drive had been projected on a screen.

"So," Chief Stowell began, squinting at the overhead projection. "What, exactly, am I looking at? What does all this mean?"

"Wish I could tell you," Trevor said, "but the files are password protected. And we have two more guesses before we're shut out for twenty-four hours."

"The feds will have been here and have confiscated everything by then," Chief Stowell said. "I'd like to get some kind of heads-up about what's come to our fair town before that happens."

"I suspect we haven't heard the last of whoever is behind this," Trevor said. "Whoever is after this flash drive, they're desperate to get it."

"This came from your brother...Marcus?" Chief Stowell asked, his brow furrowed in concern.

Aria cleared her throat. "Yessir, that's correct."

"Do you have any earthly idea what the password might be?" It seemed like the question was obvious but he had to venture an answer just the same.

"I could take a guess," Aria said, "but honestly It could be a thousand different possibilities."

"Well at least that narrows it down," the chief said gruffly. "However, you say we only have two guesses. Better make it count."

"I really wouldn't know where to start," Aria admitted.

"Marcus entrusted the flash drive to you," Trevor responded. "Therefore, he'd pick something that was obvious...but only obvious to *you*, not everyone. He would design the password to be something you'd figure out. And only you."

"In theory, I suppose," Aria said, frowning. "Hmm...Something obvious but personal for the two of us...well we tried the pro football angle, with no success. If it *is* related to sports or some kind of comic book or superhero nonsense it's far from apparent to me which one we should type in."

"You didn't know him that well, did you?" Chief Stowell asked abruptly, the look on his face revealing that hope was quickly leaving him like air from a pierced balloon.

"I once did...at least, I think I did. Anymore?" She dropped her gaze. "Not really...not as well as I wished. Not enough to know what kind of password he'd pick."

"Marcus would have thought of that, too, I think," Trevor suggested. "That you would need to have the password. Like Chief said, it would have to be something that you'd be able to recall."

"I don't know," Aria said. "He'd literally have to..." She didn't finish what she was going to say, instead considering the next few words she had been about to speak out loud: *He'd have to have written it down for me.*

Quickly, she grabbed the note and read it over carefully. "Hold on," she said, "I'm going to try and put it together."

Trevor came closer to her to get a better look while Chief Stowell stared at the screen pessimistically, his arms folded.

Three special words... her brother had written. *That's the key.*

Sibling rivalry might be the only thing stronger than carefully protected secrets. Building forts in the woods then swearing each other to keep the location confidential. One of them getting hurt during some particularly rough horseplay session and then trying to bribe the other not to tell. Discovering where Christmas gifts were being kept and selling the secret for a candy bar or a favor of doing extra chores. A thousand possibilities but only three words that provided the key.

Slowly, Aria typed *ONLY FOR US,* then thought: *That's got to be it.* She pressed ENTER.

Immediately, there was that same almost offended sound from the computer and Aria huffed in frustration. *Down to the last attempt.* Calmly, Trevor leaned forward, his index finger tapping the note on the screen. Aria read it: *One number, one capital letter.*

One number, one capital. Got it. She typed in "Only4us," then paused, her finger hovering over the ENTER key. She was holding her breath, mind buzzing, trying to decide if she dared take this final chance.

Finally, she pressed the ENTER key.

The screen flashed, the hard drive buzzing. A moment later Aria announced: "We're in."

There were thirty thumbnails on the flash drive, each ending in an mp4 format. The titles of the thumbnails were first initial/last name, apparently in regard to the subject in question whose name was listed on the drive. None of them were immediately recognizable, so Aria started at the top: *Nharlow.mp4*

After double clicking on the file, a video emerged clocking in at about forty-six seconds. Hesitantly, Aria kept the arrow hovering over the video before finally taking a deep breath and clicking *PLAY.*

As the three of them watched, a man dressed in a suit and tie approached a black sedan parked along the curb. The back window rolled down and the man appeared to have a short conversation with the unseen figure before receiving a package. The man in the suit slipped the package into an inside coat pocket and then abruptly walked away, his back to the camera. Soon after the sedan pulled away from the curb.

"What in the world did your brother stumble into?" Chief Stowell asked, almost as if to himself.

"Drug deal?" Aria asked, hating the sound of the words in her own ears.

"Maybe," Trevor said, frowning. "But I've got a sinking suspicion it's more than that. Guy was dressed pretty nicely...doesn't look like your average street thug. Click on another one."

Aria did, going to the next on the list, a *Bkoteas.mp4*

This video, timestamped at one minute and thirteen seconds, provided a bird's eye view of another transaction, this one between yet another black sedan and a limo at what looked like a warehouse complex or industrial park. This time the limo driver got out, buttoning his coat, and going to the other car. A moment later he returned, slipping back behind the wheel. The red taillights flashed before the limo pulled away. The video kept playing even as the limo moved out of the screen. The black sedan turned left, following a service road before reaching an open gate and merging onto surface streets. All the while, the camera kept track of the vehicle.

"Interesting," Trevor said. "That looks like the same vehicle that we saw in the first video."

"May not be drugs," Stowell offered, "But they're up to something awfully curious...and illegal. That's for sure."

Trevor said: "Bet next month's donuts that it's the same dude in the sedan."

Aria lacked the knowledge of how to make the picture sharper, but her first instinct was to agree with him. It had to be the same one.

"This video's a little longer," Trevor noted, "because the cameraman is following the sedan. Trying to keep it in frame until he can get a license plate number maybe."

"Hmm," Aria thought. "Well, let's check another."

One after the other they went through the videos, each file labeled with the first initial and last name of some unknown individual. Finally, at the twenty-second one, a file marked VLoenbaum, Chief Stowell interrupted them. "Hold on a minute," he said, then got on his cellphone. A moment later he passed the phone to Trevor. "Just as I thought."

"What is it?" Aria asked. "Gentlemen, please don't leave me in suspense."

Shaking his head in disbelief, Trevor stared at the screen then slowly turned it around so that Aria could lean forward to see.

"Victor Loenbaum," Trevor said. "Of Utah."

"Ernest Freeman," Stowell said, "Vermont."

Trevor stepped forward, pointing at the screen. "That one is Miss Charlene Wittenauer of Wisconsin."

Aria stared at the cellphone screen in disbelief. "They're..."

"Senators," Chief Stowell said. "And while I for one don't know how this is all connected or why your brother had this information, I think one thing is crystal clear: This whole thing goes high up the food chain, and there are quite a few interested parties that I would guess might be willing to kill in order to keep any of this from going public."

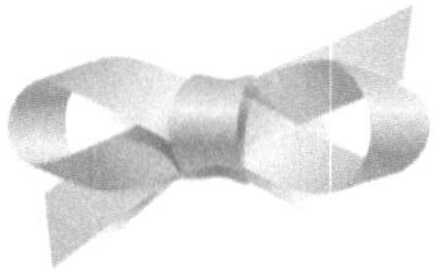

ELEVEN

The plan they came up with was a fairly simple one. Chief Stowell told them to make a copy of the flash drive and keep it secure but also to send him the videos in attachments by email. "We aren't going to give up all the leverage," he mumbled. "Especially if it comes down to a life-or-death situation. These thugs came to *our* town."

Mindful of the fact that the FBI was enroute, Stowell was doing what he could to get Aria extricated from the situation. "At least for now," he said. "Though I can't make any promises for the next few days, I'm afraid." Officer Mason, however, was another story. He couldn't get away quite so easily. Still, Aria was their priority, keeping her safe the most important aspect of the case.

"Take my car," Stowell said, "and make sure you're not followed. Make *doubly* sure, officer. Get her to a hotel up near the interstate and then get your rear back here ASAP. I'll obviously need you nearby when the feds show up."

"Yessir."

After they copied the flash drive onto yet another flash drive and followed through with the chief's e-mail, they drove the squad car by Aria's house and they both climbed out. "Let's do this quickly, okay?" Trevor asked. "Take the time to grab what you need for a couple days but try and do it fast as possible, just in case more bad guys show up."

"Got it," Aria said, heading up the walk. The weather had gotten warm enough to melt away the snow on the front walk but nothing would erase the memory of her brother's late-night visit and the subsequent break in. Even now she felt a little uneasy, her eyes darting back and forth across the street and alongside the house.

She gathered up some personal items and clothes then headed back to the squad car. Soon they were speeding back toward the police station. "Thank you," Aria said, taking Trevor by the hand. "I don't know if I would have made it if it wasn't for you."

"Just doin' my job, ma'am," he said with a grin and a pinch of his police hat.

"Goofball," she muttered to herself as she looked out the window. "Have you changed at all, Mr. Mason?"

"That's *Officer* Mason to you, young lady," he retorted. "And to answer your question: No...no, I haven't changed in the slightest."

"I figured as much."

"Do you wish that I had?"

She chuckled. "I'm not sure yet...ask me in a few days."

He grinned at her. "What makes you think that we're going to be around each other in a few days?"

"Well," she said, "because the alternative is unthinkable."

"That you won't get to see me again?"

"That we *die*," she quipped. "But, yes, I suppose I'm starting to get used to you. You've at least become bearable."

"I guess I'll have to settle for that much. For now."

The levity was welcome, but not enough to allow Aria to completely relax. They arrived at the police station, Aria half expecting to find a couple of black SUVs of the type she imagined the FBI drove. Escalades with government plates or something like that. Instead, there was just a couple of police cruisers out front, some of the constabulary involved with the library incident having since returned. "Well," she said, "our luck has held out a while longer."

"Let's not push it," Trevor said.

Hurriedly, they went into the police station then right back out the rear entrance where Chief Stowell's white Toyota Corolla was perched next to a trash dumpster. Aria tossed her travel bag—much plumper now with the extra supplies crammed inside—into the back seat and then they both climbed inside. The engine roared to life and a moment later Trevor was wheeling it around to the front of the building.

He hesitated at the road, leaning forward to peer out the windshield. He scanned the woods across the road and then looked both ways. "All's clear," he announced. "I don't think we have anyone eyeing us." He pulled out onto the road, accelerating as he headed north.

The Toyota chugged along as they made conversation. Trevor checked the rear and side view mirrors intermittently, and Aria found herself doing the same. No one had followed them out of the station, though there was what looked like a red vehicle a mile behind them that they were keeping an eye on.

"I knew your brother pretty well," Trevor said. "Though he's gotta be like four or five years older than me."

"That sounds about right," Aria said. "How'd you know him?"

"By chance," Trevor said. "Or at least good fortune. He saved me one time from getting murdered."

She shot him a look. "What?"

A crooked smile broke through Trevor's serious façade. "Okay, I guess I'm embellishing things a little. Let's just say that someone was picking on me—a whole group of boys—when I was walking home from school one day, and your brother came to my rescue."

"He was good like that," Aria said, gazing out the window. But the words she'd just spoken also made her a little said. *He was good like that, but I don't know what changed in him. He used to help people get out of trouble but then he found a lot worse trouble for himself. Only then, there didn't seem to be anyone to help him out of whatever bad thing he'd gotten himself entangled in.*

Trevor continued: "I must have been about ten or eleven at the time...that sounds about right. That'd make him fourteen or fifteen, but that's okay because the kids that were picking on me were closer to his age than mine. I remember that one of them had punched me in the stomach—knocked the air right out of me. I was crying, trying to catch my breath, my good jeans stained by the grass. They had also scattered my books all over the ground, and one of them had the audacity to have gotten into my bag of Cheetos...that seemed like the greatest injustice of all of it. I remember being afraid that I was going to have to pay some sort of fine because one of the books got a bit of mud on the pages.

"Anyways, these kids were laughing and calling me a baby and all that sort of stuff. I think one of them was about to give me another good punch—this time in the face—when your brother, Marcus Chambers, appeared out of nowhere. Standing there, tall enough to block the sun. Might as well have been an archangel come to protect me. For a while, I thought of him just like that. Like Michael, God's archangel."

"Aww," Aria said. "That's both sad and sweet at the same time."

"As it turned out, my guardian angel didn't have to fight anyone. Instead, he just stood there with his fists clenched and told them they better leave me be or they'd have to deal with him. Turns out none of them wanted to take him up on that challenge and they dispersed pretty quickly after that. I've thought about that incident many times over these years...how he stood up to bullies for some snot-nosed kid he didn't even know."

Aria was getting dewy eyed so she wiped a tear away with her finger. "He did that for me, too. But for me it was about standing up to my parents. Not that they were abusive, nothing like that. But he'd take the fall for a lot of the stupid things we'd do. For many years my brother was my hero...even more so than my dad."

"He seemed so *tall* back then," Trevor said. "A few years later and I'd just about caught up with him, but I'll never forget looking up into the sun and seeing him standing there. A living legend, the epitome of what it meant to be brave."

"Older kids always seemed so much bigger than we were back then," Aria said. "Like mythological heroes from Greek literature. Then we all grow up and they don't seem so tall anymore. Maybe it's time and trials and a whole lot of tragedy that knocks us down a peg. Marcus seemed to go through more of that than the average person but I'm not sure how much was him being a victim or him bringing it on himself. I've always hoped for the former but that's poor consolation, isn't it?"

"He's got time," Trevor said. "To change, I mean. It's like I Corinthians 13 says: Charity—what we call love nowadays—believes the best for someone. Don't stop believing that he'll come around, that somewhere deep inside is the real Marcus and that his heart is just as strong as it has always been. That he'll be back, in more ways than one."

She nodded. The truth was she *had* continued to carry that flame, never losing faith in God *or* her brother. Never believing he was past the point of no return...that the stone-solid fact remained that her Heavenly Father could reach further than her brother could ever run.

Into the silence she said: "I remember that rose you gave me during the Valentine's fundraiser."

Trevor groaned, rolling his eyes in mock exasperation. "Uh-oh...here we go."

"It was so cute. I know you were only two years younger than me but when you're really young like we were two years seems like a very big age difference, you know? But even then I thought you were cute. Your black hair, pulled so neatly to one side. Like a kid brother I never had."

"Great," Trevor said, hitting the steering wheel lightly with a fist. "Just what I was going for: Kid brother."

Aria laughed. "As you said, things change. You changed. You grew up. I looked at you differently after that."

He glanced at her; all pretense gone. "Really?"

"Yeah. Maybe I should have said something."

"I'm the one who should have said something, but I guess part of that scared little kid hung on through adolescence. You always made me nervous. Self-conscious. You were..." He took a deep breath, shook his head. "Never mind."

"Please, Mr. Mason—sorry, *Officer* Mason—go on."

"I guess it wasn't anything that could be helped. As I said, you headed off to college to pursue being a vet and I followed suit a couple years later with delusions of following Hollywood's version of a cop. I'd say we were ships passing in the night, but it's more like you were a shooting star, here today to blaze across the dark sky and then gone tomorrow. Thought I might not ever see you again. I certainly didn't think you'd come back here to good ol' Anderson Crossroads."

"Well," she said, taking his hand. "I'm here now."

He looked down in surprise, then directly at her, his eyes wide and questioning. The conversation had arrived at this point quite unexpectedly, just as the road of fate often took the traveler to unplanned—and often times *uncertain*—destinations.

"When this is all over," he said softly, "then I'd like to take you on that date. A *real* date. Do you think that'd be okay?"

"I think it sounds wonderful," Aria responded, a hint of wistfulness in her voice. "And I wonder what took you so long to ask."

To that question Officer Travis Mason had no answer.

When they reached the interstate there were two choices for hotels: One was a run-down one-story inn with fading white paint and a blue sign with the words VACANCY on the sign board. Not only was it dilapidated and forlorn, but it faced the road at the stoplight for the onramp. Too high in visibility, too low in quality, it was a failure on both counts.

A half mile down was a better option: One of those two-star, three-story franchises with interior entrances only, and a well-kept lobby with keen and sharp-eyed receptionists. There were many more cars parked here, the occupants of the hotel perhaps drawn by the promise of the free hot breakfast, heated pool and jacuzzi, or the reputation of the chain itself. At any rate, it seemed a better option. They pulled into the covered carport and Aria went inside while Trevor kept a look out over the light flow of traffic passing by. A few minutes later and Aria returned with a key card for a room on the third floor.

They drove around to the back side and Aria gathered her belongings before they went inside and took the elevator up to the third floor, the only one keeping them under surveillance a small boy dressed in blue swim shorts with a hotel towel draped over one shoulder staring up at them as if they'd just arrived from the Moon and not a neighboring town. "Hope he doesn't squeal," Trevor quipped after the boy had gotten off on the second floor and scampered toward a distant room.

"They all squeal," Aria said. "That's why I didn't bother packing a swimsuit."

At the room marked *326* Aria swiped her card and then they were stepping inside a room with a queen bed in the center, a medium-sized TV taking up part of the counter in front of it. Seeing the TV immediately reminded Aria of all the damage her "visitors" had done at her home, and she felt a swell of anger rising like an ocean wave.

"Get yourself settled," Trevor said. "And I'll sit down in the lobby for a while and make sure no suspicious looking characters like our old friends Laurel and Hardy come sniffing around."

"Okay. Thank you."

"No problem," he responded. "I enjoyed your company, circumstances notwithstanding."

"Me too."

He took a look around the room. "I hope this is suitable enough."

"It's perfect," Aria said.

"I'll call you once I learn more about what the feds want to do. I'm sure, despite all of Chief Stowell's efforts, that you'll have to come in and make some kind of statement at the very least. But we'll do our best to keep you as much out of it all as we can."

"Whatever it takes will be fine," Aria said, taking a deep breath. "I'll hunker down for tonight at least. Keep my face out of sight."

Trevor glanced at the alarm clock on the bedside table. "When you get hungry I'd advise just using Door Dash or something. There's a bunch of options around here—I saw a Pizza Hut, McDonald's and a Taco Bell when we came down the road. There's probably some other places if you want something a little fancier than that."

"I'll keep it in mind," Aria said. "Though I'm not sure I'm going to be hungry at all. I do plan on sleeping pretty hard though."

"I hope you do. At any rate, keep your receipts because I'm going to try and get all of this covered. Maybe the feds can pick up the tab."

She waved him away. "Either way, I feel safe and that's the main thing. Thanks for making sure that I'm okay."

He nodded, then looked around the room one last time. He seemed torn, but then Aria realized what his hesitation was all about. Leaving might feel a bit like abandoning her, and after all that talk about what her brother had done he hated to think about her being vulnerable and him being miles away.

"I'll be okay," Aria said. "I promise."

After a moment he sighed and nodded. "Okay. I feel better that you're here rather than in town. I have no choice but to go back. Stay out of sight, okay? Order delivery if you want some food and have them bring it to the lobby. They can call you and you go down and get it. Sound good?"

"Yes."

"All right then. I guess I better go." He turned around and headed out the door.

"Trevor?" She asked.

He paused at the door, one hand on the knob, and looked back.

Uncertainly, she looked at her bag and then the window before going to him. She took one of his hands in her own and looked up at him, her eyes searching. "I can't tell you enough how grateful I am. I..."

"This? This is nothing. It's the very least I could do under the circumstances." He shook his head. "If anything ever happened to you, I'd never forgive—"

This time it was her turn to interrupt. She let go of his hand, reaching up and cupping his cheek with it. Balancing on her tiptoes, she closed her eyes and brushed his other cheek with her lips. Then she looked deeply into his eyes. "You better take care of yourself, too, okay?"

Blinking, he nodded and let a smile crease his face. "Always. I'll see you soon."

"I'm counting on it."

After Trevor left she sat on the edge of the bed, processing the events of the last couple days. It all seemed like a dream: Her brother showing up out of the blue, her house being torn apart, the shootout in the library and her rapping a bad guy on the head with a fire extinguisher. *Okay, maybe "rapping" is a nice way of putting it...you darn near smashed it in like an overripe pumpkin.* There were good things that seemed pleasantly surreal as well: The gently drifting snow, the service at church, the delivery of the foal. Trevor Mason. Yeah, reacquainting with Trevor Mason was the best of all of it. If nothing else, she'd hold on to that part especially.

A little later she turned on the TV and clicked her way between weather stations and sports stations and sitcoms. She found *It's a Wonderful Life* on a classic TV channel and sat back to watch it. It was less than ten minutes into the movie and would provide what she felt would be a perfect diversion. But her stomach was beginning to nag at her too.

She scrolled through different options for dinner and finally decided on a chicken salad, afraid that anything else might upset her stomach. She ordered it and a bottled water through a delivery app and typed in instructions for it to be left at the reception desk.

About thirty minutes later a notification chimed on her phone. Her food had arrived. She slipped on her shoes, made sure she had her key card, and ventured out to the elevator. She was alone this time on the ride down.

She made her way past a crowd of scurrying kids on their way for an evening swim and found a friendly staff person waiting for her. "Mrs. Chambers?" She asked.

Aria chided herself for using her real name. "Yes...that's me."

"Here you go." The receptionist handed over a plastic bag.

"Thank you," Aria said, turning to go. As she did a broad-shouldered man with slicked-back hair and a pencil-thin moustache entered the lobby. He had on a black suit and gray tie and was gazing at her through a pair of spectacles. Aria looked past him to the carport, but there was no vehicle in sight. Her heart began to climb up into her throat.

The man's heels clicked as he walked across the shiny marble floor. His eyes remained upon her, the hint of a smile turning up the corners of his face. Slowly, he reached into his suit coat.

Aria backed away, clinging to the plastic bag with white-knuckled fear. The man in the suit was still walking toward her, pulling something shiny and black out from his pocket.

She wanted to turn, to scream, but it was too late for any of that. In her peripheral Aria saw the receptionist straighten, then her voice followed a moment later. "Mr. Torres," the receptionist said. "So good to see you."

The man withdrew the phone then broke his gaze from Aria, regarding the receptionist with his full attention. "Tiffany," he said cheerily. "I didn't know you were on this shift."

"Yep, afraid so." She started clacking on the keys of her computer. "Do you have your reservation number, sir?"

"Yes," he said, Aria all but forgotten as she hurried toward the elevator. "I believe it is right here."

Her stomach was troubled regardless of what she'd ordered, though the salad was bland and the bottled water unoffensive. Her nerves were frayed, and the "run-in" with the motel guest who she'd mistakenly assumed might just be an assassin was the instigator. She forced down a few bites and a few gulps of water and couldn't eat or drink any more. *It's a Wonderful Life* played out its story but even as the end credits appeared on screen Aria still felt unnerved and distracted. She shut off the TV and changed for bed. When she reappeared, she shut off the TV and the main room light. She crawled in between the cool sheets and balled a pillow up beneath her head. Closing her eyes, she tried to sleep but her thoughts troubled her. She imagined arctic winds and needles of icy rain and a car sluicing sideways over the slick road before plummeting down a snowy embankment and into the silvery scar of a frozen river.

Please, Lord, she prayed in the silence. *Give me peace with the past. Let me somehow put the accident out of my mind without dishonoring my memory of David.*

Finally, sometime after eleven, she was able to surrender to rest, though she kept the bathroom light on just the same...just like she used to do when she was a kid.

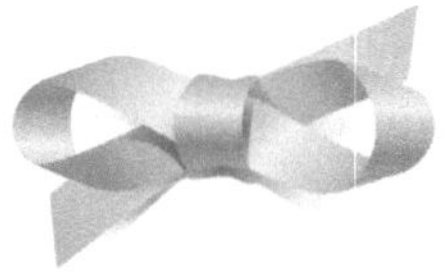

December 24th
TWELVE

The harsh morning sunlight speared through a gap in the burgundy motel curtains, cutting through her slumber. Grudgingly, Aria turned over and stared at the bedside alarm clock for a while as she tried to decide whether she had the fortitude to get up or if she'd just go back to sleep. Finally, she tossed the covers away and sat up, feet flat on the floor, rubbing at her forehead with one hand. She was not excited with what the day might hold. *I just want to escape...jump in the car and drive for a long, long time.*

That, of course, was not in the cards so she yawned, stretched, and got moving, making her way in the half dark to the bathroom where she flipped on the light and began to get ready.

Continental breakfast in the hotel lobby was an adventure of jockeying for position in line for self-made Belgian waffles, fruit and yoghurt while avoiding children scurrying under foot like eager mice. There were an assortment of listless donuts and moldy pastries on offer as well, but Aria settled for snatching a packaged muffin in between the milling crowds and then a fresh cup of coffee from the station near the front desk where a pot was simmering. She turned in her key card and then sat down on a couch to wait for Trevor.

He arrived at the hotel in his squad car just after eight o' clock. Aria met him outside as he pulled under the portico, two coffees in hand. As she got in the passenger seat he said: "Good morning, and thanks for the coffee! How'd you sleep?"

"Good enough, thanks." She handed him one of the coffees. "And you're welcome. Though calling this watery concoction 'coffee' might be a bit of a stretch."

Trevor took a sip. "My dad used to say if it wasn't thick enough for a spoon to stand up in the middle then it was too weak."

Aria smiled. "Sounds like something a dad would say. How was the rest of yesterday?"

He pulled away from the curb, shaking his head. "I would sum up my day in one word: *Long*. The Feds sent in their crew of course, but the Special Investigator—guy named Vincent Mabry—was the real gem."

"Oh yeah?"

"Yep. He wanted you there last night. Actually, he demanded it, but Chief Stowell and I held our ground. I wouldn't even tell him where you were— (I kept it intentionally vague)—but that we'd make sure and bring you in first thing this morning. He was complaining about getting things wrapped up so he could get home for Christmas Eve." Trevor glanced at her. "Between you and me I think he's planning on robbing a bunch of houses in Whoville."

"Well, I'll agree with him in one regard," Aria said. "It'd be nice to get all of this behind us."

Trevor glanced at her. "Have you heard from your brother?"

"No. I sure hope that, wherever he is, he's doing okay."

They drove under the I-80 overpass and then Trevor leaned on the accelerator as they headed toward Anderson's Crossroads. The trees along the road were still garlanded with snow, though it was apparent that it was slowly melting away. The blacktop itself was dry, the sun already climbing into another azure sky. "This used to be my favorite time of year," Aria said. "I just wish the circumstances were a little different."

"There's still time for the forecast to change," Trevor said. "Did you hear we might get a little snow tomorrow?"

Aria nodded. She had caught that on a news station while she was getting ready that morning. "A white Christmas sounds perfect."

"Yeah, Bing Crosby would then finally be able to stop moping about it."

She frowned, casting a comical look at him. "You leave Mr. Crosby alone."

They drove along, the road humming under their tires. "I'm sorry you got involved in all this," Trevor said, "but I'm not sorry I got to see you again."

Aria looked over at him. "Me too. And remember that you told me you'd go to the Christmas Eve service tonight. Don't forget."

"How could I?" He grinned.

Trevor's cellphone buzzed and he extracted it from a coat pocket. Aria listened to the one-sided conversation, and when he disconnected she asked: "The Chief?"

He nodded. "The one and only. Wants to know our ETA. Seems like the Grinch—otherwise known as Special Investigator Vincent Mabry—has been like a fly buzzing in his ear all morning. I told him we're about ten minutes out."

True to his word, Officer Trevor Mason was pulling into the police station right at the estimated time, nudging the cruiser in between the Chief's Toyota and a hulking black SUV with government tags. He shut off the engine and glanced at Aria. "Well, let's get this over, huh?"

She took a deep breath and nodded, getting out of the car. Together they walked up the front path and stepped inside the police station.

Chief Stowell was standing near the front desk, a Styrofoam coffee cup in one hand. Though obviously frazzled, he looked visibly relieved to see them. A look of grim resignation on his face, he gestured with the cup toward the station's conference room and Aria and Trevor followed, their own coffees in hand. From within they could hear a muffled voice barking orders. As the chief opened the door, Aria finally caught a glimpse of the famed Vincent Mabry.

He was standing in the middle of the room, hands plunged in his suit pant pockets, gesturing toward the screen upon which one of the video feeds that they had been viewing the previous day was frozen. Mabry was a balding and portly man of about fifty, his face grizzled by two-day growth. Neither short nor tall, neither handsome nor homely, he looked somehow more *average* than Aria had expected. Like just another guy you'd see in line at the sandwich shop or seated across from you on the bus. His suit was rumpled, his pants mismatched, a sprig of hair stuck up in an unruly cowlick from the brushed dome on the back of his head. But his eyes were fiery with what she first took to be either indignation or intensity...or a combination of both.

Chief Stowell made introductions, to which Mabry gave little response. His focus was fixed on Aria, though, like a Rottweiler eyeing a mailman who was approaching the front gate. He was chewing furiously on a piece of gum as if trying to punish it. He grumbled: "I do hope you have the flash drive, Ms. Chambers. The *original,* is what I'm talking about. It's evidence. I'm a long way from the field office in Omaha and I sure would like to get back home before it gets dark."

"I have it," Aria said softly, reaching into her purse and passing it over.

"Great," Mabry said. "You will be debriefed here shortly, but first we're going to review these files privately to see what we have. I don't need to tell you but I will just the same: None of what you've viewed or what is talked about in here is to go past these four walls. Understood? File it away in your mind under provisions of 'national security' if that helps."

"Understood," Aria said, standing there rigidly like a toy soldier.

They were escorted out of the room, Chief Stowell giving Aria a sort of apologetic look. Trevor gestured down the hall and a moment later they were in his office, Trevor seating himself behind his desk and Aria taking the chair across from him. "What's next?" She asked.

Trevor shrugged. "I'm not sure but I imagine it'll take them a little while to sort some of this stuff out. Unfortunately, they've kept me relatively out of the loop other than making sure I get you here with the flash drive."

"As long as we're done well before six o'clock."

He raised his eyebrows at her questioningly.

"I have a date," she said, "and I'm not going to miss it."

He smiled. "Glad to hear that. I wouldn't miss it for anything either."

After a while Trevor got them fresh refills for their coffees. As they waited they mulled over the case.

"Did you get any kind of read on the case?" She asked. "I mean, anything that you can talk about?"

Trevor thought that over. "They're real antsy about this whole thing. Just like Chief said, this goes way up the chain."

"Hmm...I wonder how far?"

"I wouldn't be able to truthfully say that I know the answer to *that* question, but the one I find more compelling is how the people on those videos are connected. That's where the real crux of it all lies."

She leaned forward. "Explain."

"Okay. So... the senators—and whoever else is in those videos—is one thing. A very *serious,* and even earth-shattering revelation, politically. But don't you feel like there's something even more serious going on behind the scenes? Like...well, like this is a collection of videos being used by some unseen figure...call him a sort of puppet master...to keep them in line, to do his or her bidding?"

"A conspiracy."

"Yes. And a conspiracy is even more serious than evidence of corruption. Conspiracies are things that have a lot of arms with hands reaching into a lot of places whose inhabitants wish to be left undisturbed. Conspiracies like this are extensive, in other words. Those hands go into a lot of pockets and pull triggers and do favors, all at the behest of some nefarious group."

Aria was thoughtful. "And if this is a conspiracy involving some important political figures than an even more important figure is behind it all."

"A lot of people on the Naughty List," Trevor said.

"Except the *good* kids are the ones who are supposed to get presents." Aria settled back into her chair, mulling it over. Trevor was hunched forward, his hands folded in front of himself, his eyes wide and alive.

He continued in a hushed tone. "There are two ways that dirty business gets done in Washington, right? Either by blackmail or bribery. As far as I can tell, both of those methods are in play. The characters on the video—these dirty senators—are obviously taking bribes. But at the same time, they don't know that they're being set up—*blackmailed*—by whoever is taking the video...at least, whoever has orchestrated the surveillance."

"Your Puppet Master," Aria said. "As in the one who's actually pulling the strings."

"Correct. I'd venture to say that there is a very good chance that the shadowy figures offering the bribes *and* using video evidence of it as a means of blackmail are one and the same...or, at the very least, two different tentacles of the same octopus."

Aria thought about that for a moment. "Someone is going through a lot of trouble to keep these people—these secrets—in line."

"You bet they are. I just wish I knew how your brother factored into all of it. I'm sure that's a good portion of the questions that will come your way during this so-called debriefing."

Aria groaned. "I wish we could just get it over with. I really have no clue how Marcus factors into this, and I really don't want to drag him into it any more than I have to." She shook her head. "Actually, now I'm glad he left so he doesn't have to answer all their questions."

Trevor gave her a questioning look. "He's not involved in this, Aria. He can't be. If anything, he's a whistleblower of some type. Stumbled onto this whole thing."

"That doesn't make me feel any better about it. It just means he's in more danger than we knew. Come to think of it, even Marcus probably has no clue how much danger he is really in."

Trevor looked down at his hands. "He won't get very far, I'm afraid. Something this big..." He spread out his hands. "Well, surveillance cameras are everywhere and they'll be using facial recognition, ATM tracking and whatever else they have at their disposal to hunt him down. I'm afraid it's just a matter of time."

Aria nodded solemnly. "If only I could find him first." She had texted him several times in the past couple days, asking how he was doing. He had yet to reply.

Trevor stood, folding his hands behind his back as he turned to look out the window. "If you warned him they could consider that obstruction of justice. And when terms like 'national security' get thrown around, the laws and issues of personal rights become really hazy."

"Yeah..." Aria frowned in frustration.

"I don't like it any more than you do," he said. "This guy Mabry—his whole team. To me they're just acting as cogs in the machine. Whatever is going on, it stinks of government corruption. I hate that we're stuck in the middle of it."

"Can Mabry be trusted?" Aria asked. "Am I going to get renditioned or something? Trevor, I'm getting worried..."

He turned and leaned down, putting a hand on top of hers. "I won't let them railroad you, no matter what. Don't trust them as far as you can throw them, but trust me, okay? We'll figure it out."

"This is deadly serious," Aria thought, looking down at the Styrofoam cup she held in her hands. "If they brought in a team like this to a little town in the middle of Nebraska, that means I'm in big trouble. My *brother* is in trouble."

"I don't know," Trevor said. "You gave them the flash drive, which is what they were after. They're going to question you and then let you go. At some point, though, your brother is going to have to testify. I don't see any way around that."

Closing her eyes, Aria thought about the last time she'd seen Marcus. He had looked really scared, and now she was starting to feel the weight of all his worries settling over her. *Suffocating* her. "I don't care what happens to me as much as what happens to Marcus," she said. "If he testifies and someone comes after him..." She let the rest drift off but her mind hastily filled in the rest for her: *It isn't a matter of "if," is it? ...it's already happened. They came after both you* and *Trevor.*

The incident at the library wasn't about whoever was after them trying to follow up on some details. Those men had guns; they had fired at her and Trevor in a public place...and Trevor was a police officer. Thugs like that would stop at nothing to silence the voices of those who had something to say.

Aria considered something, her eyebrows knitting together in concentration. A moment later she asked Trevor: "This Special Investigator Mabry...he didn't come with his team yesterday?"

"No," Trevor said. "He arrived this morning."

"I thought he said he was out of the field office in Omaha."

"Yeah. But he indicated that he flew in from New York late last night and someone drove him here this morning. Tried to say that that was why he was so irritable, not that anyone here believed that."

"So, his team arrived before him?"

Frowning, Trevor considered this. "Come to think of it now, there was a liaison. Chuck? Kirk? Can't remember his name. Wait a minute...um... *Clark*. It was a guy named Clark, but that was his last name. Agent Clark. He said something about being a liaison with the field office out of Omaha. I talked to him a little last night but didn't see him again. Next thing I know this Special Investigator Mabry shows up and takes charge."

Aria did not respond. Her brow furrowed even deeper in concentration.

There was a knock at the door and Chief Stowell poked his head inside. "They're ready for you," he said.

"Great," Aria deadpanned, rising to her feet and joining Trevor as they followed the chief to the conference room.

"Just relax and answer their questions as simply and truthfully as possible," Trevor said. "Everything will be fine."

Aria cast him a sideways glance as they entered the room. *I hope you're right.*

"Thank you for joining us," Mabry said, leaning against a table. He seemed a little calmer now, more even keeled. Gone was the fire in his eyes, the reddening face. He had slipped on his business façade, like a molting snake. "Please," he said, gesturing to one of the chairs facing the screen. "Have a seat."

Aria complied, sitting down, and folding her hands in her lap. She averted her gaze away from Mabry but when the Special Investigator began to speak her gaze drifted back to him.

Mabry took a long, drawn-out breath. "Ms. Chambers," he said softly, "let's just start at the beginning, shall we? Give me your account of all that has led to this moment in time, starting with your brother's arrival in Anderson's Crossroads."

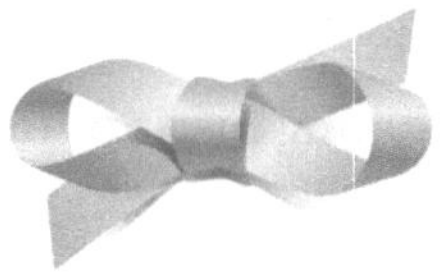

THIRTEEN

Aria started at the beginning, sharing her account of coming home to find her brother Marcus hiding in her house like an outlaw. How he had appeared desperate and in fear for his life. How they had both stayed at a neighbor's house— (Aria did not give specifics here)—before Marcus disappeared at some point during the night or early morning. How Aria had arrived home to find her own house had been ransacked. Mabry had grilled her about the details of those events but she managed to sidestep the more sensitive areas—the areas she wanted to keep private. As such, she did talk about the flash drive that Marcus had left but did *not* mention the note, nor the perfume he had given her as both a Christmas gift and a vessel to which he could attach the note.

As the questioning continued a part of Aria reminded herself that Chief Stowell had already been told about the note. She hoped that he was keeping his own cards close to his chest. Glancing at him at one point, she saw only a face as stoic as Rushmore, but she prayed that Stowell could indeed be someone they could trust to keep the necessary secrets out of play.

She progressed in her discussion through the week from that first night to the morning following. How Officer Mason had picked her up and taken her to the library.

"So, you did indeed examine the content of the flash drive?" Mabry asked, folding his arms over his ample chest.

"Yes. I wanted to see what it was all about."

He nodded. "Understandable, I suppose, though I would remind you once again that the contents of that flash drive are extremely confidential. Matter of national—"

"Security," Aria supplied. "Yeah, I got it."

"So, please, go on," Mabry said, settling his rump against a desk, his arms still folded.

"Trevor—Officer Mason—and I, we were online at the library when something caught Officer Mason's attention. What turned out to be some very bad men spotted us, came after us in the library. One of them shot at us and that's when the place went crazy. People were running here and there. We managed to get down into the basement—which ended up being kind of a trap—and were able to somehow fend them off."

"You killed them?" Mabry asked, his face set in a mask of concern.

"No, but they were incapacitated. The reinforcements arrived and took over from there."

"I see. Please go on."

"Don't you already have all this information?"

Mabry offered a plastic smile. "We're just gathering evidence and testimonies so that we can have a well-informed, detailed overview."

She spread her hands. "Well, that's it. That's about all of what we know. Officer Mason was gentleman enough to get me a hotel room in order to keep me out of harm's way and here we are."

Mabry mulled this over, glancing at one of his men before turning back to her. "All right," he said. "Anything else...are you sure that's it?"

Aria nodded. "That's everything, though believe me I wish I could fill in some of the gaps."

"So, you have no idea at all where your brother might be?" Mabry asked, treading over familiar ground. "He have any friends or family within reasonable driving distance from here?"

"My parents live in Arizona," Aria said softly. "He could be heading there, I suppose, but I doubt it. Unfortunately, there's been a falling out between them over the years with regard to his...well, his drug problems." She didn't like admitting that, especially to a room full of strangers, but she also realized it might be a way to keep the Feds from sniffing around her parents' home. *Just what they'd need after all they've gone through is a bunch of FBI agents asking questions about their son. Besides that, it's not really fair to Marcus, either. As far as I'm concerned he should be considered innocent until proven guilty.*

It sobered her to realize that the possibility of his innocence was becoming more and more a stretch, but she owed Marcus whatever loyalty—and protection—she could give him. Besides that, she had no clue what friends he might have between Nebraska and Arizona. There was literally no telling where the next couch for him to sleep on might be found.

Mabry assessed her with cold, flat eyes. Like he was attempting to use them to pry apart the pages of the secret journal that was her past. Aria resolved anew to not let him do anything to disrupt that bond she had with her brother.

Regardless of how frail the relationship had been over the years, she had to fight for whatever remained of the fragile bond.

"What else can you tell us?" Mabry pressed; his eyes fixed on her like a snake's on its prey.

Aria held her palms out open, fingers spread as if in an offering. A gesture indicating that she had nothing she was trying to hide. "That' it. I have nothing else. Not that I don't *want* to tell you, it's just that I have no idea why we're in this situation to begin with. Why someone is trying to kill me or what my brother might be involved in." That, at least, was the simple truth of it all.

Silence descended on the room as Mabry chewed it over. Finally, he mused: "Your brother, he's in a lot of trouble with the law. More than that, though is that fact that he is in mortal danger. Do you understand that?"

She nodded numbly, looking down at the floor. *Of course I do. I'd have to be an idiot not to have figured that out.*

"If you don't help us, that danger is going to be an ever-increasing reality, Ms. Chambers. Do you understand that as well?"

She nodded. "Yes. I do. That fact has been made abundantly clear to me when those hoodlums tried to kill us in the library." She exhaled, her breath ragged. "Believe me, I wish I could do more, bring this whole thing to an end. To feel safe again in my own home." That, also, was a simple truth.

He studied her for a moment longer, the butterfly under the microscope. "And you've never seen these two men before...that is, they didn't look familiar to you?"

"Not at all."

"Out-of-towners?"

Aria nodded. "I've lived here for a while and I think I would recognize them if they were locals."

"Fair enough."

He considered her for a moment, his head cocked slightly, arms folded. Finally, he sighed and turned away, plunging his hands back into the pockets of his suit pants. "Thank you for your cooperation, Ms. Chambers. I'll excuse you for now."

Aria blinked. *That's it?* Cautiously, she asked: "But, my home..."

"It's not safe yet," Mabry said. "But soon. Give us a little time as we continue to try and figure this out."

"Thank you, Aria," Chief Stowell said, giving her the clue that she was being dismissed.

Aria glanced at him and nodded. She started for the door but stopped with her hand on the knob. *Don't...* her mind whispered.

She turned around.

Let it go...

"Can I ask you a question, Agent Mabry?"

"Sure," he said.

She stood there, staring at him, wondering if she should go on. She glanced at the other federal officers who were either looking at her with expressions of mild curiosity or weren't paying much attention now at all. Finally, she said: "How did you know about the two men?"

He considered this, cocking his head and frowning. "Ma'am?"

"The men in the library..."

"Yes, I know what you're talking about but I don't understand. You are the one who told us about it…just a few moments ago."

She kept her gaze level. "I mentioned the men, but I never said there were two of them."

He held her gaze, his face going to granite, his eyes narrowing. "I just assumed…"

Aria thought about that for a moment but then shook her head. "No, I don't think so. This Special Agent Clark that was here would have filled you in on all the details before he left for whatever unknown adventure he'd been called away on. I'm pretty sure the FBI is pretty good about that kind of thing. Face it, you didn't even know that the thugs—the *two* men I mentioned—had been hospitalized. Something tells me that's a vital point that would have gotten passed along. Unless…"

"Unless?" Mabry asked.

Trevor stepped forward. "Unless you're not who you say you are."

Mabry fumed, pushing away from the desk and stepping up into Trevor's face. Trevor flinched a little but stood his ground. "How dare you…"

Now it was Chief Stowell's turn. He closed the distance, intervening between the two men. "Hold on, gentlemen. This can all be resolved with one quick phone call. After all, I've got Agent Clark's number right here."

"Please do make that call," Mabry said, hoisting up his pants. "Then maybe we can get this insubordinate deputy of yours a little time off so he can find himself another job."

Chief Stowell had fished his cellphone out of his pocket and was examining his list of past calls. "Hold on...here it is." He pressed a button, holding the phone to his ear.

Aria and Trevor kept their eyes glued on Mabry. The Fed's eyes ticked to the right, connecting with one of the other men in a look that would have been imperceptible if they hadn't been watching carefully.

Then everything went crazy.

The agent closest to Stowell slammed the butt of his rifle into the chief's skull, and Stowell sunk to the ground like a pile of laundry. In the process he dropped his cellphone and it went skittering across the floor.

Mabry whipped his pistol out of its holster and aimed at Aria's head, but she was already diving behind the chair. Trevor slammed into him a second later, Mabry squeezing the trigger reflexively. As the gunshot rang out, Aria scrabbled across the floor, the chairs providing insufficient cover.

Chief Stowell had managed to raise himself up on his hands and knees, his vision swimming as he fought to retain enough consciousness to clear his own gun. Spotting him, one of Mabry's men stepped took two steps forward, aimed, and fired before Stowell was able to slide his own weapon out of its holster.

Aria whimpered as three shots in rapid succession echoed deafeningly in the small room. Trevor had thrown Mabry up against the desks, the impostor FBI agent trapped beneath them, and now was kneeling, using a toppled desk as cover as he sighted the gunman that had brought down the chief.

Desperately, Aria scrambled toward the door as gunfire erupted around her. Behind her, Trevor fired his gun and there was a cry of pain as the other gunman fell.

"Come on!" He yelled. He rushed toward her, threw an arm around her, shielding her as bullets ricocheted off metal. They were about ten feet from the door, crouching low to the ground, surrounded by two other shooters who were wheeling around, guns in hand. Mabry was struggling to right himself, his own gun clutched stubbornly in one hand. *We'll never make it,* Aria thought. *We're going to die here.*

She peered over Trevor's forearm in time to see Mabry cumbersomely squat behind the table near the screen, breathing laboriously as he positioned his elbow to support his gun hand, the muzzle pointed in their direction. His hand was shaking, the barrel erupted, and she saw a flash of fire—as close an analogy of her life flashing before her eyes as anything had ever been in her life—and then the bullet whizzed by her ear.

Leaning tighter into Trevor's side, she shouted: "We're not getting out of here! If you try for the door they're going to bring you down!"

Frantically, Trevor looked left to right, snapping off a shot as one of Mabry's men rose from his cover near the window. Mabry fired again, the bullet burying itself in the wall behind them. "We can't just wait here, either!" Trevor responded. "We're vastly outgunned. We gotta find a way to—"

Suddenly, the door busted open and two police officers filled the gap. They were firing wildly back at the other gunmen, crouching down as they entered the room. In an instant Trevor was pulling her forward and they were ducking behind the officers, suddenly in the hall, the cacophony of gunfire exploding within the room. They spun, colliding with the opposite wall. Aria looked around frantically, trying to regain her bearings.

Trevor grabbed hold of her by the shoulders, pushed her in the direction of the front door. "Run!" He yelled.

She didn't need to be told twice.

Aria bolted down the hall and out the door, Trevor right behind her. They turned, sliding on the mushy grass, and then aimed for Trevor's cruiser. Jumping in, he punched the door locks and Aria climbed inside. He gunned the engine, the cruiser fishtailing as they arrowed toward the road. Behind them the door burst open, a few stray bullets whizzing haphazardly, but one managing to shatter the side mirror on Aria's side. Aria covered her head, ducked down in her seat.

"Hang on!" Trevor shouted.

Then they were skidding out onto the road.

Trevor fought for control as more gunfire erupted from behind them. Finally righting the vehicle, he shot down the road, heading toward town. Aria searched for her seatbelt, found it, and snapped it in place. Trevor was nudging the car up past 70 as she clung on. Trees flashed by on both sides, boughs covered in melting, glistening snow. The road was clear, there was no traffic and they had a good head start, but Aria checked the rearview mirror, nonetheless. Even with a mile of road behind them there were no pursuers on their trail. Yet.

"He's got a lot of nerve," Trevor growled between gritted teeth. Aria could see tears of rage and pain glistening in his eyes. "How many are they willing to kill to keep their secrets safe? People like my fellow officers—my friends—back there."

"They saved our lives," Aria whispered.

Blinking, Trevor nodded before swiping at his eyes with the back of his hand. "They died as heroes...Chief Stowell, the officers...all of them.

Aria reached over and lightly gripped his shoulder. "I'm so sorry, Trevor."

"Yeah. Me too."

"Right now, we just gotta put some miles between us and them. A few seconds to think."

An idea dawned upon her. "We need to go by your great grandmother's house...exchange cars. They won't be looking for mine."

He nodded his head vigorously, gripped in the vice of surging adrenaline. "Good idea," he said. "We need to make sure that we stay a step or two ahead of them."

Aria checked the side mirror, then craned her neck to look back through the rear window. There was a flash of sun on glass. Someone was pulling out onto the road almost two miles behind them. Barely visible, the vehicle would have disappeared from sight completely if the red and blue lights hadn't started dancing from the roof of the vehicle. The warbling of a siren began echoing through the air.

"Wanna play that way?" Trevor murmured angrily. "Fine." He flipped on his own siren and lights and punched the accelerator toward the floor. Aria watched as the speedometer inched above 80.

For three miles they managed to maintain a good cushion, but the pursuers were slowly closing the distance somehow, even though Trevor had the needle pegged at 85. Then, abruptly, he took his feet off the gas, eased on the brake and pushed more forcibly as a side road came up quickly on the right. He managed to take the corner without spilling them out into a ditch and then he was accelerating once more. They both kept their gaze alternating between the road ahead and behind them.

Trevor shut off the sirens and strobe lights. They hurtled down the side road, slewing left to right as they went like a bobsled on a track.

The road winded left and right. Trevor kept his speed around 45, maneuvering as best he could across the half-frozen mud, the cruiser following in the ruts of former travelers. A minute later and Aria saw a familiar sight: Her Honda, nestled under a thin blanket of snow that was stubbornly clinging to the roof. Trevor slid to a halt a few feet from it and shut off the engine.

Aria grabbed her purse from the floorboard of the cruiser as she exited the vehicle. Digging through it, she found her keys and pressed the fob to unlock the doors. Exchanging one getaway car for another, they slid into the car and Aria started it up, making sure to switch on the heater.

She backed out of the spot, careful to maneuver around the cruiser. As she shifted into drive a large mass of packed snow calved from the roof and slid down, first onto the dash and then onto the ground. There was still some snow clinging to the windows but she had enough visibility to drive.

"Go slow," Trevor urged her. "They would have caught up to us by now if they saw where we turned off."

Aria nodded, brought the car to a stop at the end of the drive. "Where do I go?"

Trevor considered that. They had barely escaped the police station and even then it had been an impulsive retreat. They were just trying to get away…there was no real plan, at least not thus far. "We should put as many miles as possible between us and them…try to contact the authorities."

"Good plan," Aria said, turning left, heading back in the general direction from which they'd just come. The sun flashed across the windshield, burning high in the sky over a realm of melting snow. That would not last long, though, she knew. Another front was slowly moving into the area if the weathermen on TV were to be believed.

"I'm afraid of what we're going to find back there," Trevor said nervously. "The chief is dead… But what about the others? I can't…" Suddenly, his voice hitched, and when he looked at Aria she saw his eyes were again shimmering with tears. "They saved us, you know? They didn't deserve any of this."

"You're right," Aria said, "but at least we know the score now. These men will do anything to keep their secret under wraps, a secret we don't even understand. It's time to bring in the big guns…Cops, National Guard…whatever is necessary."

"Okay, yeah…" Trevor was pulling out his own phone, tears sliding onto his cheeks. Even though he was a police officer, Aria had to remind herself that he had been a small-town cop…he'd never been exposed to something as crazy as what had happened at the station. In the midst of all of it he was also trying to come to grips with what was the certain loss of close friends, his fellow officers. Steeling himself for the eventual revelation of those who had died so that they could escape and keep living. *We owe them the truth,* Aria thought. *Somehow, we must bring every single person who is involved in this evil to justice.*

They made their way cautiously to the edge of the highway, Aria half expecting to see one of the commandeered cruisers or the black Escalades perched on the shoulder, awaiting their return. Instead, it was open road in both directions...not a vehicle in sight. They'd gotten away and Mabry and his thugs were most likely rolling through downtown Anderson's Crossroads at that very moment.

Not wishing to push her luck, she wheeled the Honda onto the highway, driving away from town and in the direction of the police station.

A few minutes later they passed by the station and Aria let off the gas, drifting over to the shoulder. There were still a couple vehicles in the parking lot, and the front door stood open. As they watched a figured appeared near the back corner, animatedly chatting on a cellphone, his back to them. He held an automatic rifle in his other hand, the barrel resting against his shoulder and the end pointed toward the sky. One of Mabry's thugs. For a moment, Aria imagined the real FBI team dead somewhere—in the woods or in a motel room. Slaughtered by evil men trying to cover their selfish secrets. Men willing to kill whoever got in their way in order to do so.

"Go..." Trevor whispered, as if the distant man might hear them. Aria eased back out onto the road, gradually building up speed. As far as she could tell, they had remained unobserved.

"We'll send EMS for them," Aria promised. "Let the whole US Armed Services swoop down upon them if need be. But we gotta keep going."

"Yeah..." Trevor said. He looked down at the cellphone, his hands trembling. Then he resolved himself, wiping his eyes with the back of his hand before swiping up on the phone so that the home screen appeared.

Before he could type in 9-1-1 the screen flashed alive, the title UNKNOWN CALLER appearing on the screen. Hesitant, Trevor stared at the number for a moment as if trying to decipher its source. Then he swiped the green icon and tapped the speaker button.

"Who is this?" The voice on the other end asked.

"You first," Trevor shot back.

"Vincent Mabry...we need to talk."

"You've got thirty seconds. A whole world of hurt is about to descend upon you so you better go ahead and say what's on your mind."

On the other end, Mabry chuckled. "Fair enough, partner. Listen, your girlfriend has something that I want...that I *need*. If you can deliver it to me in the next few minutes I'll be so grateful that I might let you both live. But no promises..."

"No chance," Trevor said. "Your little cover up is over. We're calling the authorities...not just the state police but *everyone*. You better get ready to sit behind bars for the rest of your life."

"Now think about what you're planning on doing," Mabry said. "Is all this hassle really worth it? The life of you or your girlfriend? Think this through, Officer Mason."

"There's nothing to think about. It's over."

"Oh, but it's not," Mabry said. "Not even close to being over, in fact. I need that flash drive or someone near and dear to you is going to get hurt."

Trevor said nothing.

After a long pause, Mabry returned: "Are you there?"

"Yes, I'm here."

"What happened at the station was totally unnecessary. We were going to talk, come to an agreement and then everything would have been over with little fuss. Then your girlfriend decided to be cute, to try and pull the rug out from underneath us. You did some damage—I'll give you that—but she ended up making things a lot messier than they needed to be. In fact, you can blame her for the death of your chief, or those fellow officers of yours, for that matter. She forced my hand, you see. It was...a necessary evil, I'm afraid. But you can blame yourselves."

Trevor ignored the barb. "Your days—no, your *minutes*—are numbered. Then you'll pay for everything you've done."

"I don't think so," Mabry said, his voice maddeningly calm. "You're both going to bring me what I've asked for and then the three of us are going to have a nice little chat."

"What makes you think we're going to turn this car around?" Trevor asked, then silently chided himself or giving away even a hint of the plan.

"Because I think you love your great grandmother too much to let her die. Am I wrong about that?"

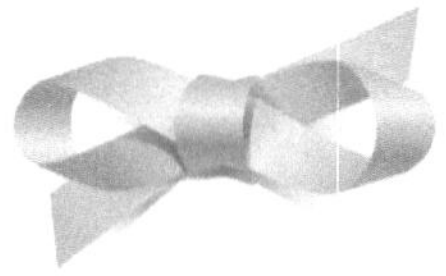

FOURTEEN

Trevor's whole body was coiled as tight as a drum as he leaned forward in his seat, the cellphone pressed to his ear, his other hand bracing himself against the dash. "If you so much as lay a finger on her..."

Aria had slowed, checking the rearview mirror before pulling over onto the shoulder. She watched him with concern filling her eyes before her gaze drifted down to the phone.

"That all depends on what you decide to do," Mabry said. "We don't want to harm her...we just want that flash drive. No one else needs to get hurt."

"You already have the information, why does the—"

"We *need* that flash drive," Mabry reiterated, his voice temporarily becoming more strained. "It's no good to you, so why don't you just turn it over?"

"I'll put it in your own words, Mabry," Trevor said. "It's evidence. Evidence that one way or another is going to help put you away for a long, long time."

"It has nothing to do with me, but as far as my employers are concerned..."

"Well then, it'll lop off the head of the snake. That's the most important thing. That those who caused this chain reaction through which my dear friends and chief have died...the terror you've inflicted on those who are innocent..."

"Nobody involved in this has clean hands," Mabry said patiently. "Not even that girl's brother...Marcus. He's on the run for good reason, you know. He's implicated in this, too."

"I don't believe you," Trevor said.

"Well, I guess whether you believe me or not, you'll have to grapple with that one. Either way, you have a decision to make."

Trevor glanced at Aria, searching for the right response. Finally, he said: "I need some time to think."

"Really? You don't want—"

"Look, pal, you're not in charge here, okay? You don't hold all the cards and there's one in particular—a really, really big wild card—that we have in our deck. You understand? The flash drive—the one you want so badly—is in our possession and will soon be handed over to the police."

"I don't want to drag this out," Mabry complained. "Let's get this over with before you or that girl you're with decide to do something stupid."

Trevor's mind raced. He glanced at Aria and held her gaze as he said: "There's a Chinese restaurant in town—west side in a strip mall. Golden Phoenix. We'll be there at noon and we'll have the flash drive. That's the best I can do."

There was a moment of silence on the other end. "Fine. General Tso's chicken and some steamed dumplings sounds pretty good right about now. All that gunplay has caused me to work up an appetite. But there better not be any cops or great grandma isn't going to be around to open her presents tomorrow. Nobody wants that kind of thing at Christmas, right?"

Trevor said nothing. He gritted his teeth angrily.

"Guess that's settled then. Noon at...Golden Phoenix. Got it. That's less than two hours, Trevor."

"I know what time it is," Trevor said.

"Perfect. Shall I order you two something? Egg rolls? Crab Rangoon? Anything?"

"How about your head on a platter?" Trevor asked. "That'd be a perfect holiday treat."

Mabry laughed. "I like that. That's a good one. Bye now."

They disconnected and an absolute silence settled over the car. Finally, Trevor ran his fingers through his hair and looked over at Aria. "Look, you don't have to..."

"We're in this together," Aria said. "I'm not going to leave you now. Besides, it's my—"

"Don't even start down that road," Trevor said softly. "Nothing about this is your fault, and as far as your brother is concerned it sure is starting to look like he was just trying to get the bad guys to pay for their evils. Keeping them accountable. Even if the jury is still out on that account I'm inclined to give him the benefit of the doubt. Why else would the bad guys be after him?"

"Thank you," Aria said, tears filling her eyes. "Your belief in him means everything to me right now."

She leaned her head against his shoulder and a moment later he brought the palm of his hand to her cheek. Looking up at him through her tears she saw that all the anger and rage had left him, leaving only a haunting visage of deepest concern. His eyes had softened, and she was plunged back through the years to the little boy that had presented her a rose at Valentine's Day. She felt a tear escape down her cheek, then one from the other. He brushed it away gently with one finger.

"It's going to be all right," Trevor whispered.

"How do you—how *can* you—know that?"

He smiled reassuringly, then turned slightly to lay a kiss upon her brow. "Have faith," he said.

"Okay," she said.

Straightening, she wiped her eyes and looked out the windshield. "I suppose we better not just sit here on the side of the road."

"No," Trevor chuckled, "I suppose not."

"So where to?" She asked, shifting into drive.

"Towards town but let's stay on the back roads. Plus, I need a little time to come up with a plan."

"I thought that the Golden Phoenix was the plan."

"That's the setting," Trevor sighed. "I'm still working on the rest."

10:43 AM.

Aria pulled her eyes from the clock and looked out the windshield. They were parked next to a car wash half a mile from the shopping center in which the Golden Phoenix Chinese restaurant was situated. Trevor had his head cradled in one hand as if trying to shield it from the sun, but they were currently parked in the shade. He was thinking. Plotting. Planning.

"We have a gun with a clip and two bullets," he said finally. "Not very helpful. I guess our greatest possible weapon right now is the element of surprise."

"They'll be waiting there to ambush us," Aria said, then shook her head. "I don't see how we're going to succeed by sneaking up on them unannounced."

"I'm working on that one," Trevor assured her. "But let me know if you get any inspired ideas."

According to the website, the restaurant didn't even open until 11:00. While they didn't have time to kill, they did have a few minutes to orchestrate a plan. They had already driven by the strip mall, Aria behind the wheel while Trevor remained hunkered down and trying to spot bad guys on the perimeter. He'd seen a pair in the parking lot sitting in one of the black Escalades and another single gunman poised in a cruiser across the street. He guessed there'd be yet another covering the alley and back egress. Besides that, there might be one on the roof, he supposed.

Trevor shifted in the seat next to her. Sat up straight, poised for action like a guard dog who had just sensed activity nearby. "What do you say we do a little shopping?" He asked her.

She started the engine. "I'm always up for a little shopping."

"Today will be my treat," he said.

There was a little plaza nearby that had a discount clothing store anchoring one end. They found a parking spot up close and went inside.

Cheery Christmas music, cloying and out of place amidst the stifling atmosphere of impending danger, floated from speakers mounted overhead. A voice cut in every few minutes announcing early closing for the holiday and last-minute specials. Dodging mothers toting toddlers and pushing grocery carts, Aria and Trevor hustled their way through the store, just two more latecomers desperate for a deal and that last minute gift for a forgotten relative.

The first stop was ACCESSORIES, where each of them grabbed a knit cap, scarf, and gloves. Then they split up to get the rest of their ensemble. In five minutes, they met back together to examine their wares: Aria had chosen a fur-lined jacket and a pair of black boots while Trevor had settled on a baggy pair of snow pants and a brown flannel shirt.

"Those do *not* match, sir," Aria said, allowing herself a moment of levity.

"I'm not going to a fashion show," Trevor said. "Besides, this is not an outfit...it's a disguise."

"Gotcha."

They went to the register where a girl in her late teens with an elf hat and faux reindeer antlers tallied up their selections. "That'll be $252.71 after tax," she said in a tired monotone.

Trevor whistled and swiped his ATM card. "What about those last-minute deals I heard about?" He asked.

The girl thrust a listless finger toward a set of sale racks about thirty feet away. "Just on *actual* Christmas apparel. You know, ugly sweaters, festive apparel, and all the stuff that only a goofy grandparent would want to wear."

"That seems unnecessarily...*mean,*" Trevor retorted.

She smiled mechanically. "Merry Christmas. Or Happy Holidays. Or...whatever."

As they exited Trevor said: "She's one to talk about goofy apparel."

Aria gave him a light slug on the side of the arm. "Okay, now, jokester. Time to get serious."

The humor was a distraction from the danger that awaited them moments later. Once they left the store and the cheery Christmas music the reality of it quickly settled over them again. Aria got back behind the wheel and started the engine.

They drove out of the parking lot and headed toward the strip mall and the Chinese restaurant.

Trevor tapped the clock on the dashboard. "It's 11:05. It might be time we get on over there."

"And you have a plan?" Aria asked.

"Of course," he said. "Follow my lead, if you'll be so kind."

They approached from the south, keeping the Golden Phoenix restaurant to their right on the opposite end of the plaza. Turning into the large parking lot, they both scanned the area carefully. Aria readily picked out the Escalade in the middle of the lot, watching it out of the corner of her eye. She looked across the parking lot for any other signs of surveillance but couldn't readily find anything.

Trevor directed her to the alley, and she carefully drove behind the buildings at a slow crawl. Trevor leaned forward, searching for any sign of one of Mabry's men positioned back there. A moment later he spotted someone loitering near the fence, squatting down next to a trash dumpster, and smoking a cigarette. "There," he said. "We better turn around."

Aria complied, braking, then going into an awkward K turn in the narrow alley. Finally, she got the Honda pointed the other way and exited the alley, emerging into the parking lot once again.

"Like I figured," Trevor said, "there's going to be only one way in."

Aria looked at him. "What way is that?"

He just stared at her for a moment before smiling. "Park the car."

Aria dutifully parked the car in an empty slot. "We need to act casual," Trevor said as he exited the vehicle.

"And what is it that we're doing, exactly?" Aria asked.

Trevor just gave a nod toward the roof. "Coming in the only way they don't have under surveillance. This is gonna be a surprise party we're throwing for our friend Vincent Mabry."

At the side of the building, they found a caged ladder mounted about eight feet off the ground. Aria gazed up at it, shaking her head. "No way I can reach that," she said. "With these boots on I'm still only about 5'9."

"I'll hoist you up," Trevor said, "unless you want to stay in the car. In fact, I would definitely prefer it if you stayed down here but I've found that you can be rather stu—"

"Hoist me up," she interrupted him. "You're not going in there alone."

"As you wish," he replied, scooting over next to the building. He formed a foothold with his interlaced fingers. Aria took a quick look around before putting a hand on his shoulder and stepping up into the foothold. A moment later and he was hoisting her up toward the ladder. She grabbed on, dangling there as she tried to find her footing against the smooth side of the building. Finally, she managed to scramble up and into the enclosure.

Backing up, Trevor took a few deep breaths and then took a running leap for the ladder. He caught the first rung but then lost his grip, tumbling toward the side of the building. Aria was staring down at him. "What's wrong?"

Trevor rubbed at a shoulder, wincing. "Not as young as I used to be, and not as athletic as I remembered. Just...just hold on a second."

"You're like twenty-six," Aria chided him, unable to contain a chuckle in spite of the *gravity* of the situation.

He tried again, managing to hook one set of fingers over the bottom rung before hanging there like a chimpanzee in an enclosure. Straining, he grabbed hold with the other hand and summoned all his might to perform a single pull up. Somehow accomplishing that feat, he grabbed hold of the next rung with one hand, his feet scrabbling against the bricks. With a little effort he was able to join Aria on the ladder and they began their ascent.

One after the other they climbed up the ladder and onto the roof. From here they could barely see the tip of the Escalade, which was good news because it meant they could proceed unobserved. Hunched over, they began to hurry along the roof, dodging antennas, and other obtrusions as they made their way toward the other end. Even from here Aria could spot the box indicating a stairwell near their destination.

When they arrived there they found the door unlocked, but stuck. Forcing it open, Trevor slipped through the gap and Aria followed. They could hear the clang of pots, the rattle of silverware and the sound of voices drifting up from below. A set of rickety stairs were at their feet, spiraling downward. Aria nudged Trevor to take the lead, and so he began down, trying to keep every sound to a minimum.

On the ground floor they found themselves in an alcove cluttered with crates full of produce and a variety of boxes of canned goods. Big white bags of rice were regimented against the wall like toddlers waiting to be let into class after recess. Waiting for her eyes to fully adjust, Aria observed that they were standing in a narrow hallway, the restaurant's kitchen on one side and an adjoining business on the other. Ahead of them was a single glass door that gave way to the dining area. "Here we go," Trevor said softly.

They passed by the kitchen, a few cooks casting confused looks in their direction but not making a fuss out of their presence as they tossed rice and vegetables and chicken in woks. The smell was intoxicating, but Aria tried to keep her mind on the task at hand.

At the door, Trevor reached forward carefully and put his hand on the lever. He pressed down, easing it open. Immediately they were greeted with the sound of non-festive music and the rush of water from the little koi pond that Aria knew was positioned near the entrance. They hesitated, looking around for Vincent Mabry.

"A man like him never sits with his back to the door," Trevor murmured. "He'll be against the wall on one side of the dining room. I guarantee it."

Aria said nothing, keeping right at Trevor's back as he ventured further into the room. A waitress rushed by with a soft drink in each hand, headed for a couple who were seated at a table on the other end of the room. Then both Aria and Trevor spotted Mabry, who was indeed seated in a booth with his back against the wall. For now, he hadn't noticed them. He was too busy dipping a dumpling in soy sauce. Seated next to him was a tall man in a white, buttoned shirt. The man's eyes widened as Trevor shot forward, closing the distance between them with surprising speed.

The man next to Mabry reacted quickly, bringing his gun up from the table, but before he could clear it Trevor was already there, shoving the barrel of his own gun into the side of the man's neck. Slowly, the gunman placed his pistol on the table.

His mouth half full, Mabry sputtered and dropped his fork. He grappled for his glass of water, spilling a good portion of it on the table. Slurping a few gulps, he set it back down and looked at them aghast. He attempted to maintain his composure as he offered them an embarrassed and crooked smile. "You're...you two are early." He coughed roughly. "What...what a pleasant surprise."

Trevor jabbed the barrel of the gun harder into the gunman's neck, his expression strained as Aria snatched up the man's pistol and swiftly dropped it in her purse.

Vincent Mabry analyzed them both in turn before regarding Trevor with an amused look. "So...indulge me a little. You snuck in here unawares, which is very impressive. But what's your plan for getting *out*?"

Trevor lowered his gun as a waitress approached. He held it low at his side, nudged against the gunman's leg.

"Hot tea?" she asked, oblivious to the nature of the customers' "discussions."

"That would be lovely, thank you," Trevor said, trying to sound calmer than he truly felt.

"I'm good," Aria said.

The waitress gave a little bow and disappeared back into the kitchen. Mabry watched her go, his face smug and his expression one who had never lost control of the situation for even a moment. It angered and unnerved Aria at the same time.

"Your plan?" Mabry repeated.

Trevor leaned forward and Aria thought she could sense a hint of trepidation—like a fleeting shadow—pass over Mabry.

There and gone, little more than a flicker in his eyes. "My plan," Trevor said, "is to fix this whole mess. Like I said over the phone, we're calling the cops and you and your crew are going to answer for...for all of this."

Mabry chuckled. "You're both really in over your heads, you know." He selected another dumpling, spearing it with a chopstick before dipping it into the little bowl of oily sauce and bringing it to his lips. "What you're up against can't be stopped. The wheels are in motion, the locomotive is barreling down the track. You might as well try and stop a boulder rolling down a steep hill with one hand."

"I don't care what this is all about...I'll let the feds—the *real* feds, not murderous imposters like you—figure out all that political stuff. I'm here to take you to them."

"You should care, you know," Mabry posited around chewing. "It might just be what you refer to as 'political stuff,' but I assure you that it impacts you both directly. As I said, it's way beyond stopping now...the proverbial runaway train is gaining momentum and once it goes off the rails everyone will feel the tremors as it crashes."

Trevor pressed his lips into a thin line. "As I said, I don't care about all that."

"Aren't you a little outmatched?" Mabry asked. "By my count it's six against one. You being that one, of course, with your pea shooter there. Of course, all that can change in a snap of the fingers."

Trevor narrowed his eyes. "The next call we're making is to the police."

"And what about your great granny? Are you so willing and ready to just dispose of her like tossing an old carpet in a dumpster? Does her life mean so little to you?"

"Be quiet!" Trevor said. "I won't take moral advice from you, of all people."

"Okay, but answer that first question at least, Officer Mason. What about ol' granny? I feel like she's the wild card here...I should say, *my* wild card." He spread his hands. "Looks like we're at a bit of an impasse."

Trevor gritted his teeth. "Being at an impasse would assume that we are in a mutually vulnerable position. But we're not." He pressed the gun harder against the thug's leg. "I would have you call off your goons but I don't trust you. So, instead, you're going to go with us on a little trip."

Mabry chuckled. "What makes you think I'm going to go along with this?"

"Because," Trevor said. "If you don't, I'm going to put a bullet in your friend's knee. I'm sure it'd be quite painful."

Mabry shrugged it off.

"Then you'll be the next one on the list, but I'll aim a little higher."

Again, there was a flicker of something in Mabry's eyes...there and gone as quick as a bird passing in front of the sun. Aria couldn't tell for sure but it looked like fear...at the very least, uncertainty. Then the man 's face cracked into a cold, predatory grin. "I'll cry out of course. My boys will come running."

"I don't mind taking that chance," Trevor said. "I don't mind continuing to put bullets in various body parts until you respond accordingly. Until you comply."

Mabry watched him for a long moment then finally shrugged. "Fine. But I'm going to get what we came for. One way or another."

A thought struck Aria's brain, and she said: "What is, exactly, that it is you came for? The flash drive? Something easily copied and sent as an attachment? An eventuality that you could certainly assume has already happened?"

Mabry said nothing, took a sip from his cup of tea. He offered her a smile.

Aria assessed him carefully. *It's like gathering feathers from a pillow being shaken out in a hard wind...you can't win that game, can't cover something like this up. So, what really is your angle?*

It also occurred to Aria in a fleeting moment that maybe the flash drive wasn't even the most important thing he was trying to recover. But what else could it be? She forced herself to remain focused and dispelled the thought.

"Let's go," Trevor said, jamming the gun into the other man's leg. "Nice and slow."

For now, at least, the man complied, sliding slowly out of the booth as Trevor had directed.

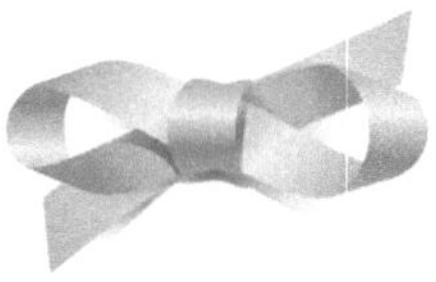

FIFTEEN

Trevor and Aria led Mabry out through the kitchen, then to the stairs. If the kitchen staff of the Golden Phoenix noticed them at all, they gave no indication. The waitress stood near the back door as if to block their escape, arms folded and tapping a pen against her cheek. She gave them a withering stare until Trevor fished out a twenty-dollar bill and handed it to her. Then she smiled, gave a little nod, and ducked out of the way. *She still doesn't know what's going on,* Aria thought. *She just didn't want us to leave without paying. Well, that makes sense.*

Alone now, the trio mounted the stairs, Mabry in the lead with Trevor jabbing the gun into the base of his spine, Aria bringing up the rear. Their footsteps clomping upwards echoed in the narrow shaft. Soon enough, they had reached the door to the roof. Trevor sidled by Mabry in order to pry the door open. Fresh, cold air blasted them in the face.

"What're we doing up here?" Mabry wondered aloud. "Are you guys planning on throwing me off the roof?"

"Don't tempt me," Trevor said, "though I'd rather see you come to justice...pay for your sins."

Mabry shrugged as if it was no big deal to him either way. He shuffled forward, his eyes drifting left to right. *I don't like this,* Aria thought, looking around to make sure they were still unobserved.

"If you don't want to talk about what you're after," Aria said, "then maybe you can just tell me how my brother figures into all this."

Mabry gave a scoffing chuckle. "Your brother? He's a nobody. A delivery boy who is in way over his head. If you think he had any idea about what was going on, then you're fooling yourself. What a joke."

"Then why are you after him?" Trevor demanded, pushing Mabry forward. "Why won't you leave him—and Aria—alone?"

Stumbling, Mabry righted himself and shot Trevor an angry glare. "I'd hate to ruin your image of him..."

"Go ahead," Aria pressed.

"Fine. Your brother, as I just said, was nothing but a delivery boy. A delivery boy that decided to run off without doing what he was paid to do. It was such a simple errand, too."

"So, he owes you money?"

Snorting, Mabry turned around. He began to laugh as if Aria had just shared the funniest joke he'd ever heard. "This is about money, you got that part right, but it's not about money *he* owes *us*. Though..." Mabry spread his hands. "I guess he does owe us, now that you mention it. $10000, to be precise. But that kind of money..." he shrugged, raising his eyebrows. "Eh, that's not really what it's all about. There's something much more valuable than that which Marcus can..." Mabry stopped mid-sentence, as if he'd said too much and was about to say even more.

Aria's head jerked in his direction. *Marcus owes these crooks $10,000, more than enough to get him killed, but it's not about the money? And he was about to say that Marcus still has* *something very valuable that they're after. That's not the flash drive he's talking about. Then what could it be?*

After a moment, Aria said: "What does he have? Help us understand and maybe we can get it back."

Mabry looked up at the sky, wincing. As if to ask God to help him out. "Look, he's got some...some *information* that we need. You better hope—for his sake—that he still has it."

As they walked along the roof, Aria considered the videos they'd watched of politicians in high places receiving what looked like bribes. Mabry had not been concerned about the fact that those files could be transferred quite easily by a few keystrokes and an email. He wasn't bothered by that. At the same time, it always came down to money and power with politicians and the dark corners they'd be willing to go to in order to rub shoulders with another type of power.

Then it hit her. If the files with the bribed politicians on them weren't being used for leverage since Mabry didn't seem to care about the flash drive, then it meant that what happened to them was inconsequential to Mabry and his goons. It might present a devastating threat to the politicians, but that part of the equation was over for Mabry and whoever employed him. It wasn't about leverage, it wasn't about the payouts and it wasn't even about some connection that could be drawn to Mabry, his employers, or anyone else who had dealings with the politicians. *These guys don't work for the politicians...they can all get hung out to dry as far Mabry is concerned.* It was about whatever was on the reciprocal end of the deal. The politicians had gotten their gifts and now Mabry's employers were looking for their Christmas presents...what—and who—they paid for.

Of course, there was no way Aria could know what it all amounted to.

Information, not money, she thought. At the same time, they would probably kill Marcus just out of principle, maybe making him the fall guy first. Ultimately, they wouldn't hesitate to kill all three of them if they had the chance. Aria was under no notions to the contrary of those simple little facts.

The trio eventually made their way across the roof to the ladder at the base of which the Honda would be waiting for them like an obedient dog. When they got there Trevor grabbed Mabry around his upper arm. "You go first. And don't try anything. I'll have my gun trained on you the whole time."

"As you wish, your majesty," Mabry said with a smirk. Holding onto the ladder, he slipped one foot down to the first rung, eyeing Trevor with solemn malevolence but saying nothing more. Soon he was over the side and descending.

Trevor glanced worriedly at Aria. "I'll go next, make sure that Mabry doesn't try any crazy stunts. Once I'm over you follow, okay?"

Aria nodded. "Be careful," she said.

Trevor followed Mabry, the gun in his right hand and trained downward, stepping delicately into the void with his back to the rungs. His left hand held onto the railing behind him as he went.

Aria stepped forward, gazing out over the edge. Even though they were only about twenty feet off the ground by her best estimation she felt vertigo spinning her world sideways before she regained control. She closed her eyes, refocusing, then reached out for the railing.

The metal was cold under her fingers, the air fresh and clean. Below her she could see Mabry climbing down, Trevor awkwardly tracking him from a few rungs above. She turned, gripping the metal with both hands as she dangled a foot over the edge like stepping cautiously into a cold pool.

Suddenly she saw a blur of movement from the other end of the complex, and it took her a moment before she realized that it was at the stairwell of the Golden Phoenix. The door had come crashing open, a flash of metal winking in the sun. A figure burst forth, staring right at her while clinging to something in his hand.

A gun, she realized, making the connection a little too slowly. In the split second of her delay the figure had lowered the weapon, aiming it toward her and squeezing off a shot. She had a horrified moment, paralyzed at the top of the ladder, to see a flash of gunfire—the second time that day—and then a second later the bullet pinged off the metal less than six inches from where her hand gripped the ladder.

She cried out, half in alarm and half in surprise, then ducked down. The figure was running toward her now at a full sprint, across the roof, his arm coming around for another shot.

"Trevor!" She exclaimed. "Trevor...there's a gunman on the roof!"

Trevor looked up in surprise. By now he was halfway down, Mabry below him a few feet. Aria worked her way down from the roof, turning her attention from the gunman to Trevor. To Mabry, who was only four feet from the ground and suddenly leaping off the ladder.

"Trevor!"

This time Trevor needed no direction. He gazed down as Mabry landed on the asphalt, rolled away and darted toward the Honda. Trevor held his fire, turning and shoving the pistol into the waistband of his pants, clambering down as quickly as possible. Mabry was running toward the parking lot.

There was the sound of another report from the gunman's weapon and a chunk of brick broke off over Aria's head. She ducked as powder and chunks of the brick cascaded over her. These, she realized in a moment of terror, were no warning shots. She and Trevor were open targets. They had been called to the Golden Phoenix not for a negotiation but to be assassinated. That fact, if hazy before, was resolving into a thing of crystal clarity now.

Trevor dropped to the ground and turned, drawing the pistol as Mabry disappeared around the corner. He took up the chase as Aria continued to descend. She reminded herself that somewhere above the gunman was closing in on them fast.

From an unseen location came the screech of tires. Trevor had reached the corner of the building and now slid to a halt, backing up and turning. "Aria!" He shouted. "Hurry...we gotta get to the car!"

Aria knew that the gunman on the roof was about to appear over her at any moment. She took a quick glance at the remaining distance to ground level—about six feet, she figured—and took a careful leap, turning first and then pushing off from the ladder, arms held out to her sides like wings. She readied her legs to take the impact, praying that she wouldn't twist an ankle or do something worse. That she would be able to fold just right as her feet connected with asphalt. Somehow she managed to land square, but the collision from that height was jarring, nonetheless. She bent her legs on impact, absorbing the worst—but not all—of the landing. She stumbled forward, fell onto her hands, and then popped up almost instantaneously to her feet. She stole a glance at the roof but no assassin had reached the edge yet.

Turning, she landed in Trevor's arms, who had arrived at that precise moment. Scooping her up, he guided her toward the Honda. Behind them came the sound of an engine roaring.

Then gunfire. Aria ducked down reflexively as Trevor squeezed off two rounds toward the roof, where the gunman had suddenly appeared. Aria ripped open the driver's door and slid behind the wheel of the Honda, fumbling with the keys. Trevor continued around the front of the vehicle, snapping off shots at the rooftop gunman as he made his way to the passenger side.

There was a shriek of brakes and Aria lifted her eyes in time to see a limo rolling into view. It skidded to a halt and the doors flew open. Before she could see a single face there were muzzle flashes and gunfire erupted into the air. She sunk lower toward the floorboard as the windshield imploded, sending shards of glass showering over her.

"We need to get out of here, Aria!"

Turning her head, she found herself looking into Trevor's wide eyes. Bullets ricocheted off of metal, tore through fabric and dimpled the side panels of the poor Honda. Trevor held the gun in his hand but in the midst of the onslaught it was like wielding a toothpick in a sword fight.

Aria fumbled with searching fingers until she found the automatic start and jabbed the button. The Honda's engine roared to life and Aria began scooting up a little, mindful of the fact that the rooftop gunman could appear at the side of the car at any moment and she'd be crouching there without any option for escape. Completely vulnerable. T

We have to get moving. Right now.

She shifted the gear into drive and pressed down on the gas with one foot. The Honda shot forward, but Aria was driving blind, her head still well below the dash. A volley of bullets pelted the car as it advanced, and a moment later there was nothing but the sound of the Honda accelerating. Only then did Aria attempt to shimmy her way up to catch a glimpse of where they were headed.

Right at a tree.

She jerked the wheel to the left, accelerating as a few stray shots zinged by the car like angry wasps. Then they were hurtling through the parking lot, dodging stationary vehicles and last-minute shoppers puttering along. A few of these leaned on their horns as the Honda shot past them.

"What now?" Aria asked, frantically searching for the exit to the lot. "Where do I go?"

"You choose, Aria. Just *go...*"

She figured that was a good enough plan for now. She skidded out onto the road, taking the path of least resistance to the right. Rubber squealed, the smoky smell filling her nostrils as the car righted itself and shot forward like a cat. Trevor chanced a look over his shoulder. "We're going to have company here in a second," he muttered. "I'd advise you to keep the pedal down...go as fast as you safely can."

Aria nodded her head vigorously, thinking about the contradiction between "fast" and "safely." Regardless, Anderson's Corners was not a large town and in a few seconds she had gotten through what passed for the commercial district and was speeding through the residential areas. She glanced in the rearview mirror and saw a pair of black vehicles weaving through traffic, a quarter mile or so behind but closing the distance quickly. *This time I don't think we'll be able to outrun them. But let's do our best, Aria.*

She slid into a turn onto a side street then punched the accelerator, the engine roaring as the Honda quickly climbed back to sixty. A yard sign flashed by on the right: *PLEASE DRIVE AS IF YOUR CHILDREN LIVE HERE...* She felt a little guilty as they rushed on, but there were no children in sight on this cold day and it was a life-or-death mission besides.

"Aria..." Trevor groaned, pointing.

She saw it too late. They hit a speed bump a moment later and went airborne, Aria fighting to control the vehicle as it slammed roughly back down. She felt like her teeth would rattle out of her skull. But she didn't so much as feather the brake pedal, mashing down on the accelerator as she flew through a stop sign.

The pair of black cars, single file, drifted around the last turn, not so much as shimmying as they swooped after them. *Professional drivers,* she thought. *What chance do we have of escaping?*

She yanked the wheel to the left at the next street and then on impulse veered back to the right, sliding into an alley between houses as Trevor hung on for dear life. "There's only one place we should go," Aria said through gritted teeth. "Your grandma. We need to get her before it's too late."

"They'll be expecting that," Trevor said. "Besides, if he already has someone posted there, we'll be driving right to our own deaths."

"But..." Aria was frustrated, fighting the wheel as it drifted through icy patches in the alleyways. *How did we arrive at this point, to things getting so way out of hand?* The simple answer was her brother, but she wasn't ready to make him the target of her frustration and anger. Not yet. If he was guilty of something—bringing this upon her, Trevor, and anyone else who was innocent and had gotten caught up in the whole thing—she wasn't ready to be the one to sit in judgment, at least not yet. There were still unknown elements that had eluded them thus far.

"We need a place to hide out for a moment," Aria said. "A place to think. If we can just shake them off our tails first."

Trevor looked over the back of his seat in time to see the first of the two black cars backing up. They had missed the pursuit through the alley and had also lost some distance on the Honda. *Great job, Aria! Score one for the good guys.*

Marcus was always complaining about the cops giving him a hard time. But he'd brought a lot of that on himself. Right now, there were no cops to call...none who were local, at least. The only one who could help was sitting next to her and was in just as perilous a situation as Aria herself was in. There was no one to run to, not now...it was just them and they'd have to figure it out for themselves.

"Any ideas?" Aria asked.

"I'm working on it," Trevor said. He was staring down at his phone. "But keep going. You're doing great."

Emerging from the alley, Aria slowed just enough to make a sharp turn back to the right, the car shuddering and then sliding and then grudgingly yielding back control. They were now returning the way they had come, back toward the commercial district by of an alternate route. She knew that beyond the surface streets was the highway that would take them out of town. Open blacktop—covered with a little snow and ice, of course—and miles and miles of road bordered by trees and barren fields. More the second than the first.

Trevor was talking to someone, and it took Aria only a moment to realize who it was. A guy name Edward who was a caregiver at the assisted living place where Trevor's great grandmother resided. "Yes...listen, Edward...yes, Olivia Mason, my great grandmother. You need to listen, okay? You need to get her out of there. She's in danger. No—I can't explain all that right now, but someone is coming to kill her and I need you to get her out of there if you can. Use your vehicle, take her out through a service entrance. Yes, that's right. Cops? There are no cops, but I'm working on that. Yes...thank you. Do it now. Don't ask anybody, just get it done. Thank you, Edward!"

He hung up, stared out the windshield as one hand braced against the dash.

"She okay?" Aria asked.

He nodded. "So far. North Platte is a ways from him and I'm gambling on Mabry's threat being a hoax. But if not, I pray it's not too late. I hope I didn't make a major mistake, one that proves fatal for Edward." He ran his fingers through his hair, then turned his attention back to the phone. "I'm going to get the state police on the line...I should have done this a long time ago but things got so...hectic."

Aria watched the road. Their options were evaporating, the only positive point right now that they had, at least for the moment, lost their tails. Somehow, Aria knew that victory would be short lived. At the same time, she was mindful of the fact that a junction was coming up in less than a mile. On the other side of the commercial district was a bisecting county route that speared through flat lands and eventually led to Peter Dillahunt's veterinarian office.

A part of her felt that they were being pulled magnetically in that direction, but another part of her didn't want to possibly get Peter or his wife embroiled in all of the danger. These were really, really bad men. Dangerous. And they had a lot to lose. A few bodies in the snow would not stop them...it wouldn't even slow them down.

She glanced at the fuel gauge. They had a quarter tank, which would be enough for a while. At the same time, they certainly couldn't run forever. They could try and leave town but the bad guys would anticipate that...might even have someone waiting somewhere for them down the road. If they didn't get away or find somewhere to hole up for a while then they were going to die. It was as simple as that. And the clock was ticking.

If we lose them they'll have no idea that the Dillahunts is where we're headed, she thought, trying to assuage her conscience.

"I've got an idea of where we can go," Aria said, almost too softly to be heard. Next to her, Trevor nodded before beginning to converse with the state police.

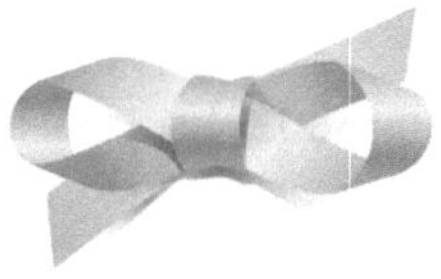

SIXTEEN

"The police are on their way," Trevor said, visibly relieved as he got off the phone. "A whole convoy of troopers should be rolling into town within the hour."

"And your great grandmother is safe?"

"Edward just texted me. They are going to meet as at the Dillahunt's, though it will take them a while to get there. I told him to make sure there were no tails—especially black SUVs—and to take back roads once they come off the highway from North Platte. I think..."

"Dare we say it's over?" Aria asked, letting out a tired laugh.

"If not yet then soon, at least," Trevor said, glancing in the rearview mirror. "Looks like you've shaken whoever was on us a while ago." He grinned at her. "That's some fancy driving, lady."

She shook her head. "It's amazing what a little desperation and adrenaline can do."

"We might have a spot for you on the force."

"No thanks," she said. "I've had enough adventure the last two days to last a lifetime. I'll leave the rest of it up to the professionals."

Trevor grinned at that. "This is more action than I've had the entire time I've been on the force in this little town," he said. "Hasn't been this exciting since the Yarmouth incident."

"Yarmouth incident?" Aria asked. "Do I even want to—"

"Yarmouth was a rookie with the department a little over a year ago," Trevor explained. "Emphasis on the *was*. Couldn't wait to join the force, to get out there and catch him some bad guys. He had initiative, energy, and dedication. I'll give him that. Unfortunately, what he was shot on was common sense."

"Really?" Aria asked. "Okay, now I'm intrigued. Gotta hear the rest of this."

"Dylan Yarmouth. I can still see his face clear as day. Anyways, we get this call from an older lady here in town. For the purposes of confidentiality, I will leave her name out of it."

"Fair enough."

"We'll call her Ms. Doe. She's in her seventies or eighties, widowed lady who lives with her three cats. She calls 911 about one of the cats being stuck—not in a tree, but in the attic. Somehow little Mittens got squeezed in a spot where she couldn't get out, and Ms. Doe couldn't get her out either. The poor cat was just writhing in there and hissing and whining.

"So, I show up right when Deputy Dylan Yarmouth pulls up in his cruiser. Together we go to the door and knock and Ms. Doe lets us in. She then proceeds to show us the general area where the cat was stuck.

"Yarmouth reaches in the other end, straining, and gets his fingers all the way in the tight spot enough that the cat bites him. He yanks his hand back out like he touched something really hot. Well, in the process he trips on one of the trusses, falls backwards, stumbling, and lands on his backside between the cross beams. When he lands the ceiling gives way—he goes plummeting through the ceiling and lands in the bathtub one story down. Fiberglass, splinters of wood, you name it. He lives a big, jagged, Dylan Yarmouth-shaped hole in the ceiling."

Aria laughed. "You're kidding. Was Ms. Doe mad?"

"More surprised than anything. She only gets irritated later on when a contractor comes in to give her an estimate on the repairs. Long story short, Chief Stowell makes Yarmouth pay for the damages."

"You're kidding."

Trevor shrugged. "That's kinda his way I guess."

"Did you all ever get the cat out?" Aria asked.

"*I* did, yes," Trevor said, shaking his head. "Remember, Yarmouth was downstairs taking a soak in the tub. But, yes, I got the cat out after getting my hands and arms all scratched up."

"So, the story has a happy ending then," Aria observed with a crooked smile.

"For the cat? Sure."

"And Deputy Yarmouth ended up quitting eventually, or..."

"He was fired," Trevor said, "for discharging his firearm at a Bingo parlor when the crowd got a little feisty. But that's a whole other story."

They continued on through the country. Aria and Trevor would alternate glancing in the rearview mirror, but the road behind them remained as empty as the winter fields stretched out on either side of the Honda. Against the odds, it seemed that they had escaped.

They hooked a left at a crossroads and continued another mile until the Dillahunt estate came into view. Soon enough they were taking the winding driveway up to the house. This time both Peter and his wife were on the porch, looking at them quizzically.

"To what do we owe this pleasure?" Peter Dillahunt asked. "I told you we had off for the holiday. I didn't expect to see you back for a couple days, Aria."

"I'm sorry about the intrusion, but we didn't know where else to go. You know Officer—"

"Mason. Of course." Peter cocked his head. "And please don't think of this as some kind of imposition. But what brings you to our neck of the woods?"

"I'm afraid it's a bit of a long story," Aria said.

"Come inside, you two," Mrs. Dillahunt said, waving them forward. "It's a little too cold to be yacking out here."

As they mounted the porch Aria began to explain the events that had transpired the last few days. She went through it like reviewing bullet points at a staff meeting. As she talked, Mrs. Dillahunt's eyes grew exceedingly wider, repeating the phrase "oh, dear" over and over again like a mantra. Peter Dillahunt listened intently as well, but more stoically: He had his arms folded, his eyes narrowed not in suspicion but with an intense concentration. Midway through Aria's explanation, he excused himself.

"I hate that we came here," Aria explained again. "But there was nowhere else to go. We made sure—no, doubly sure—that we weren't followed."

Mrs. Dillahunt nodded reassuringly. "Yes, dear. And not to worry...you're safe here."

As if to punctuate that point, Peter Dillahunt returned a few moments later lugging several black and pea green canvas bags in hand and slung over his shoulder, like an overburdened traveler. Slinging them down, he began to unzip each one in turn, describing each weapon as she withdrew them from the satchel.

"We have a bit of an arsenal here," Mrs. Dillahunt explained, almost apologetically.

Aria observed the collection of guns. "No kidding."

Mrs. Dillahunt sighed, as if Peter Dillahunt's exhibition of guns for guests was not an uncommon practice. "Not that we ever thought we'd have to go to war. It's just..."

"Best to be prepared," Peter said. "But don't discount the possibility of a war suddenly breaking out, either. I was listening to the news the other day and the commentator they had on said that he thought—"

"Peter," Mrs. Dillahunt interrupted softly. "Now's not the time for your conspiracy theories."

"Conspiracy theories? I just..." Letting the thought go, Peter adjusted the glasses on his nose and glanced sheepishly at his guests. "No, I guess it's not." He stood back, admiring the guns that were now spread out on the couch. "Well, you can take your pick."

Trevor laughed. "Hopefully we won't need any of those. The state police are on the way."

"Well, that's fantastic news," Peter said, awkwardly taking his seat next to his wife. "So now we just wait and see?"

"That's about the gist of it," Trevor replied. "I'm so thankful that you all are letting us hole up here until they arrive."

Peter waved him off. "Think nothing of it...nothing at all. We're glad you all came to us." He snatched up a TV remote and turned it to a news channel. "Let's see if this whole thing has any coverage yet."

Shaking her head, Mrs. Dillahunt said: "Of call places, Anderson's Corners...and on Christmas Eve! Can you imagine?"

"Believe me," Aria said, "It's much more excitement than I could have planned this Christmas."

Trevor excused himself to the kitchen, where he got the state trooper he had talked to before on the line. Aria joined him, standing next to him where she was able to glean most of the conversation. As Trevor got off he glanced at her with a reassuring look. "They should reach town in the next twenty minutes. Looks like order will be restored once more."

Aria exhaled. "That is...oh that's such a relief! And hopefully Edward will be here soon, also."

Trevor nodded, taking a look into the living room. Without a word he ventured to the door, gazing out the glass screen window. The sun was high in a cloudless sky. "Soon," he said. "They should be here at any moment."

Aria went to sit down as Trevor monitored the front drive. About ten minutes later a car slowly came into view, gliding up the road before slowing at the end of the Dillahunt's driveway. Peter Dillahunt reached for one of his shotguns but Trevor waved him off. "I recognize the car," he said. "It's Edward with my great grandmother."

The driver seemed uncertain, but then turned into the driveway and meandered slowly toward the house. Trevor went outside and down the stairs to meet the vehicle, an old pale blue station wagon. Aria followed, but waited at the bottom of the stairs, shielding her eyes from the sun.

The station wagon pulled up beside Aria's Honda and a moment later a short, thin Hispanic man got out of the car and shook Trevor's vigorously. Then Trevor was embracing him, all while Edward looked around in bewilderment. "Thank you," Trevor said, repeating the word over and over again. Aria wondered if it had more to do with the risky favor Edward had pulled or for the fact that they had arrived at the Dillahunts' safely. *A little of both,* she decided.

Trevor rushed over to the passenger side and opened the door. Olivia Mason, Trevor's ninety-three-year-old great grandmother, got out of the car on unsteady legs, and stood looking around. Trevor braced her with one hand under her arm and the other gently resting on her opposite shoulder as he guided her toward the house. "Steady now," he cooed, as they took their time getting there.

"We weren't followed," Edward said, looking from face to face. "I'm almost certain of that."

Aria stepped forward, introducing herself to Edward, who still looked as if he felt as out of place as a junior high boy at a Senior prom, offering everybody a nod and a toothy grin. Then came Olivia, like a queen to her throne, mounting the stairs gingerly before being ushered into the Dillahunt house. *What a motley crew we are,* Aria thought to herself with a smile. *But safe and secure now that this is all over!*

She whispered a prayer of thanksgiving then her mind flashed to the memory of her last interaction with her brother. She added his name to the prayer, hoping with all her heart he was also somewhere safe and warm. *When this is all over, we're going to sit down and get reacquainted, fix what has caused us to drift apart.*

Inside the house a space was found for everyone, though Mrs. Dillahunt had to shoo Peter Dillahunt and his guns away.

This he did readily enough, though he kept a couple of the weapons leaning against one corner of the room just in case. This Mrs. Dillahunt tolerated with a half-serious, half-amused expression.

Peter settled into an easy chair, consumed by his fruitless search with the remote for some kind of coverage of their fair town. Mrs. Dillahunt slipped into the kitchen, promising any of the takers a hot mug of cocoa. Edward sat between Olivia and Trevor, his hands folded in his lap, saying nothing.

Aria felt Olivia staring at her. When she met the old woman's gaze, Olivia said: "Who are you, dear?"

"Aria. A friend."

Olivia seemed to try and process that as if she was just given a particularly difficult trigonometry equation. Next to her Trevor laughed and put a hand on his great grandmother's.

After a few minutes Mrs. Dillahunt poked her head in the room and said: "Peter...instead of jumping in between stations can you find something for us to watch? A Christmas movie...something?"

Peter's eyes were glued to the TV as he flicked the channels between the local and national news stations. "Yes, dear," he said, finally giving up and settling on an old, black-and-white *Christmas Carol* movie. Old Scrooge was standing in the middle of the street with the jolly ghost of Christmas past, watching the children cavorting in the snow.

"This was a Christmas tradition of ours," Aria said to Trevor. "Watching *A Christmas Carol* at some point in December. I think there was usually hot chocolate at those viewings as well. Christmas cookies if we were really lucky." She smiled at him. "Now my family is spread out in different places and we'll probably never have a chance to be together under one roof for Christmas, maybe ever."

"That's a depressing thought," Trevor said.

"Depends on the family," Edward interjected humorlessly.

She turned to Trevor. "Did you have any special Christmas traditions?"

He mulled this over. "Not per se. My brother and I would grab trash can lids whenever there was so much as a few flakes of snow and try and find a good hill to slide down. The results varied, but usually amounted to more grass and mud than anything else. Other than that, and a few gifts on Christmas morning, that was about it. Not that I'm complaining. I have such fond memories of growing up, and Christmas was at the heart of many of those."

"Dad would read the Christmas story," Aria continued. "And we would have a big breakfast...all the works: Biscuits and gravy, eggs, sausage, bacon..."

"Yum," Trevor said. "I don't know about breakfast, but now that you mention food and Christmas traditions I do believe that Dad tried to keep our Christmas afternoon Chinese food dinner a tradition."

"He loved Chinese food, huh?"

"He loved *food*, period," Trevor retorted. "Chinese was the only place open on Christmas day, at least around here."

Aria giggled, looking past him to Edward. "How about you, Edward? Any Christmas traditions?"

"At our family Christmas get-togethers, I was tasked with trying to keep Uncle John from drinking too much eggnog and tying up the bathroom," Edward said. "But, yeah, we had the gifts and all that."

Trevor and Aria exchanged a glance, Aria's fist coming up to her mouth to stifle a laugh.

"Hey..." Aria said, reaching out to squeeze his hand. Trevor turned to her; eyebrows raised. "Looks like we might just make it to that first date."

He grinned. "It does, doesn't it?"

She heard a buzzing sound and reached for her purse. Instead, Trevor was pulling his own phone up and staring at the screen. UNKNOWN NUMBER, it said. "That might be the police," he murmured. "Hello?"

Aria watched as his face transformed into a mask of concern. He stood suddenly, going to the door and peering out the window. Then he gazed back at Aria. "I understand," he said, giving her a worried look. "Okay. Yeah, just a second." He crossed the room and handed Aria the phone, an apologetic look on his face.

She looked up at Trevor uncertainly before taking the cellphone out of his hands and putting it to her ear.

"Hey sweetheart," the voice of Vincent Mabry said. "Thought I'd share the good news with you. It's gonna be a happy holiday after all."

"What do you want?" Aria demanded.

"What do *I* want? Nothing! Santa is giving me just what I asked for, and here I was thinking I'd end up with another lump of coal this year."

"Oh, just you wait. You're gonna get more than that."

"As I said, I was just reaching out to herald the good news."

"What? That you're going to drive yourself off a cliff?"

He guffawed. "That's a good one! No, no, of course I'm not going to do that. The good news is for *you,* dearest Aria."

"What are you talking about? I'm about to hang up this phone if—"

"Wait...I call bearing good tidings of great joy," he said gleefully. "Your brother is back in town, just in time for Christmas!"

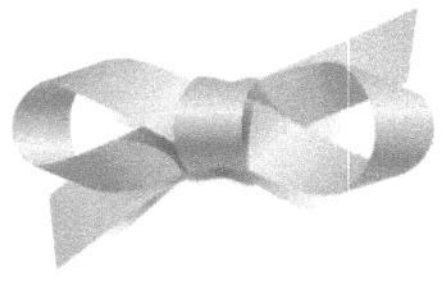

SEVENTEEN

Why, why, why, Aria thought to herself. *Why can't you stay out of trouble, Marcus? Why does everything you touch turn to ashes? Why couldn't you just stay out of sight until this whole thing blew over?*

She had hoped in vain that Mabry's call was just a ruse to get them to foolishly pop out of their hiding place and show themselves, but when Aria demanded that Mabry put her brother on the line the voice that followed was unmistakably his. If that wasn't enough, Mabry texted a photo of Marcus following the call. Her brother looked vulnerable and frightened, wide eyes above a pale face, the bottom of which was wrapped in duct tape. She had no choice now; she was being forced to comply with Mabry's instructions.

The call had ended and resignedly Aria and Trevor had explained everything to the others before exiting the Dillahunt house and going back to the car.

This time, Trevor was driving the Honda, leaning over the wheel and peering through the windshield with determination and focus possessing his features. Like they were hurtling forward toward a tornado even though the sky was clear and endlessly blue. On a mission at the end of which remained a huge question mark: Would one of them die today...or would all three? Aria had never felt more helpless, more consigned to a fate that was completely out of her control.

The situation, which seemed to be proceeding toward a happier conclusion, had fallen apart like a sandcastle in a tsunami. Everything right had been turned upside down, all semblance of order lost. They were pawns in an evil man's game and that feeling of helplessness was beyond frustrating.

Aria watched Trevor as he drove, ceaselessly blaming herself for his involvement in all of this. *I should be here alone. It's me they really want. Two of us may go down today—me and Marcus—but I needn't have involved Trevor in this zero-sum game. His death will be so unnecessary it just might drive me mad.*

A part of her mind urged her to anchor herself to her faith, the necessary spiritual response to the deadly situation. She knew that voice was right, but for now she had squeezed faith out of her thoughts, the desperation and regret and uncertainty of it all foolishly crowding out all other impulses, that interior voice—the one that cried out in panic and unloosed her moorings—screaming above the still, small voice of the Spirit.

Even now she was trying to strategize about how she might be able to leave Trevor behind. She'd choose her moment, leaving him stranded on the side of the road as she went on alone to face whatever fate awaited her. Alone, just as always. This time at least she wouldn't live to regret losing someone she cared about. There didn't seem to be any other way, did there?

Trevor was silent next to her, oblivious to her thoughts and concerned only with getting to Marcus as soon as possible. Aria began to consider that Trevor had his own strategies as to how he could put himself in harm's way and keep Aria safe. She had learned enough about him in the past couple days to realize that much. He might already have the plan of his own in place.

Certainly, he wouldn't allow her to go marching into the lion's den to face off with Mabry and his assortment of base fellows alone. Not a chance.

They had been instructed to come to the address that Mabry had shared over the phone. "No cops other than Mr. Mason," Mabry had told them. "And he better be unarmed. If I get a hint that you all are going to try something funny, or if I so much as sniff a copper badge then Marcus here is going to die. But he'll suffer first, just because I'd sure get a kick out of seeing that after all the trouble he's put us through."

Aria had no reason to think that Mabry was bluffing. If nothing else she could be reminded of the massacre at the police station. The man was unafraid to take down whoever got in his way, no matter how many casualties that entailed. There was also the fact that he had taken out a whole FBI team before arriving at Anderson's Crossroads. To say he was dangerous was the understatement of the year. He was reckless and desperate and would stop at nothing to achieve what he had set out to do.

"We need a plan," Trevor said. "We can't just walk in there like he stipulated, unarmed and at his mercy. We'd be like wooden ducks in a shooting gallery."

"Oh, I'm under no reservations about that," Aria said. "That's why we brought the guns. It's just a question of how we're going to be able to get this done without Marcus—or one of us—getting killed." *That's the $100,000 question, isn't it? It's a question you don't have any kind of answer for. Maybe that's because there is no answer to it.*

Peter Dillahunt had graciously let them borrow several shotguns and a couple of pistols for good measure, arming them like children going off to the Crusades. Aria was pretty sure that no one really thought they'd come back. Not even dear old Olivia, who had sat there stoically and without comment as they began their preparations.

What made matters worse was that the clock was ticking. They were already several minutes behind schedule. Mabry was keeping his eye on that clock, gauging how long it should take them to make the trip to town. The only card that they still were able to retain and hold close to their chest was that he didn't know what their point of origin was. Just that they were relatively close by. No way was Aria going to tell them that they were at the Dillahunt's place. It might buy them a couple more minutes before Mabry or one of his lackeys began to experiment on Marcus with sharp objects.

If there was a silver lining to any of this it was that, after some deliberation, Trevor had contacted the state police and filled them in on what was going on. He begged them to stay away until gunfire erupted or they saw the black SUVs peeling away from the location, but not a second before. "This is a hostage situation," he had explained, "and we're going to do our very best to get Marcus out of there." Their discretion would be a matter of life or death.

No matter what happened, Mabry and his goons were finished. Even if there were casualties, at least a little justice would prevail.

If we survive this, then you're going to have a lot of explaining to do, little brother.

They arrived in town, rolling through the commercial district and spotting several state trooper patrol cars on their way through. Trevor waved to these fellow policemen, driving through their midst as if leading a funeral procession. Only they were all alone. Just Trevor and Aria on their way to an unknown future. They drove past the plaza, the Golden Phoenix sign loud and proud above the restaurant like a marquee for a fantasy adventure movie. They went on, eventually passing the car wash where they had strategized a few hours before everything went to pot.

Another mile and they reached Garfield Street, and Trevor pulled right. They passed by a series of ranch houses with basketball hoops and abandoned tricycles and flags proclaiming loyalties to a variety of local college and professional sports teams. Up a hill and then over the crest, sliding through a copse of silent trees standing like guards along a promenade. Back into the country west of town with its endless fields of melting snow and long, white picket fences and cows grazing on hay. At some point Aria surrendered her anger, realizing that thoughts of vengeance and retribution would do nothing to clarify her thoughts and her focus and that the defender they needed most was with them but unseen. That there was a peace that the world couldn't give and that she wouldn't let it take away. Finally listening to that voice that cried out for her to rely upon God and her faith to keep her composed. She felt like a widow on her way to face her husband's executioner.

Long after Garfield Street became CR 170, they spotted an old oak sign that announced SWOPE ACRES, not their ultimate destination but one of the last recognizable landmarks before they reached it. They exchanged a glance as they continued on, knowing that they were in the last quarter mile of their journey.

It was here that Trevor brought the Honda to a stop.

Turning to Aria, he said: "Look, this is where I leave you to get back behind the wheel and drive back to the Dillahunts. I don't—"

Aria leaned toward him. "You are *not* going down there and taking care of a problem that is my problem...a family problem..."

"A *family problem?*" Trevor exclaimed. "Are you kidding me? That's what you want to call this?"

"Yes, it's—"

"I'm not letting you go down there, Aria. No chance, no way."

"It's not your decision to make!" She protested; her fists clenched. "This is my responsibility, and I'm going to take care of it. Look, I may not make it back but that's *my* decision to make. Marcus is my brother and—one way or another—it's all going to end here."

"Aria..."

She shook her head vigorously side to side. "You can't talk me out of this. I'll get out of this car and *run* the rest of the way if I have to. You can't—"

"I *will* stop you from going. No way is this happening." Trevor interjected. "What kind of man would I be if I just let you do that? Huh?"

"Here we go," Aria said. "Mr. Macho. Have you ever thought that maybe this is *my* life we're talking about here. You just want to intrude, and try to take over, but—" She let the rest go, realizing too late that she might have said too much.

Trevor stared out the window, his mouth agape. On the steering wheel, his hands trembled.

A moment passed. "I'm sorry," Aria said. "I didn't mean that you intruded on my life. Look, if there's anyone who I would want to be here with me right now, it's you. But you've got to stay out of this part, or you might very well get killed, and I could never forgive myself if that happened."

"What do you think I'd be doing right now, letting you go and not fighting for you to think about this? Sending you off to the slaughter...does that seem like a reasonable thing to do?"

"You or me, someone is going to be risking their life." Aria looked away. "It should be me. As I said, Marcus is my brother. I feel like I should bear some of the responsibility for what happened in his life."

Trevor shook his head, took her by the hand. "You can't think like that. No way in the world should you blame yourself for the choices he's made."

She sat staring down at her hands. When she finally looked back at him, the words she had so painfully struggled to find finally at her lips, her eyes were full of tears, one finally breaking free to slip down her cheek. She brushed it away like a snowflake, gazing skyward in an attempt to both recall the past and to keep the other unshed tears from falling. Steadying herself, she dared a look at him. "I lost someone already," she whispered. "Someone that I was close to...someone I was in love with. It has been so difficult dealing with it, for the longest time I thought I'd never attempt to find someone again. That it was better to just go through life alone, haunted by the memory of loss. To let something die inside me. At least when you're a ghost you can't feel that kind of pain anymore. But it's the not feeling *anything* that's the worst part."

He gauged his own response for a moment. The appropriate words to meet the ones she'd so tenderly surrendered. Finally, he decided that listening was the only thing he should do. "What happened? If you don't want to talk about it—"

"No, no," she said, steeling herself. "That's the thing. I *need* to talk about it. Get it out to someone I trust and maybe at the same time get it out of my system. But even saying that seems cold...like a betrayal of the dead.

"I know we haven't known each other—not *really* known each other for more than a few days. But..." she shrugged. "I don't know, I feel like you're trustworthy. That whatever I tell you will be kept safe. That I won't regret it. That you are faith-worthy, too, and that means everything to me."

"You can tell me anything," he said. "Anything at all."

"I don't really need to keep reliving the events of what happened," Aria explained. "That's a big part of my problem, why I've struggled so long to move past it." She looked at him, studying his face. "I was engaged to a wonderful man; two years ago, he was coming to visit me—it was the week of Christmas and...and there was an accident. His car slipped off the bridge into a half-frozen river. By the time the paramedics got to him it was too late. He'd just..." She left the rest unspoken. It wasn't necessary to fill in the rest because she knew it all too well and Trevor could imagine it well enough on his own.

"I'm not trying to assume anything," Aria continued. "And I'm sorry if it seems like I am. It's just. Well, you're a terrific guy. Everything a girl could imagine. I don't know if I can open myself up to someone again...at least not yet. I just don't know, that's the truth of it. But I feel like even now—perhaps because of all the crazy things that have happened these past few days or in spite of it—I'm drawn to you. Maybe we're destined to remain just friends. Maybe..." she shrugged.

"Maybe we'll just see what happens," Trevor suggested, taking one of her hands in his own. "Aria, it's okay. We'll keep this in prayer and see where the Lord leads. What else can we do?"

She thought about that and smiled. Gave his hand a squeeze. "Yeah. That sounds right. Regardless, I don't want to lose someone again. I...I just *can't,* you know? If nothing else, I've come to care about you a lot and I...Trevor, I don't know if I can stand to see someone I care about taken away from me again. It's just so hard...it's almost impossible to imagine going through that kind of grief all over again."

"I understand," he said encouragingly.

"At the same time," Aria continued, "I can't go on forever mourning him. David's gone, and I believe with all my heart he's in Heaven. He was a good man, but more importantly he was a *godly* man, and I think that's what I loved the most about him. I know where he is, even if I've lost my way a little down here." She let escape a mirthless chuckle. "Does that make any sense?"

"Sure, it does," Trevor said. "In fact, it makes perfect sense."

"Someday I've got to learn to let go," she said. "Let his memory go to Heaven with his soul. To find closure. He's at peace, it's the ones who remain that suffer the loss, who have to battle with their feelings of what was lost or, in my case, what never really came to fruition."

Trevor was silent for a moment. Then he said: "No one can tell you how to grieve. Everybody's different. One thing is for sure, Aria: The night is long and dark, and full of weeping, but joy comes in the morning."

She glanced at him, a smile playing on her lips even as the tears clung to her eyes. "Psalms?" She asked.

"Thirty, verse five," he replied, smiling. "I paraphrased it a little, but it's definitely one of my favorites."

"I'll hold onto that one if you don't mind."

"Of course. God's Word is for sharing, after all."

Groaning, she returned her gaze to the stillness outside. There was a fence bordering the property at the top of the hill and she examined it now as she tried to sort through her thoughts. "You really aren't going to let me go down there, are you?"

"Not a chance," Trevor said. "I'm sorry, but it's non-negotiable."

She blew her hair out of her eyes in an act of frustration. "And I'm not letting you go down there, either."

He gazed at her, a slight grin on his face. "I'll run the rest of the way."

"I'll run you over," she said in response.

"Not if I take the keys."

"You wouldn't..."

"They're already in my pocket."

Aria gave him a steely glare, though there was no anger in it. All of that anger had leaked out like air from a balloon. "Trevor..."

"What?"

"All right, fine. We're at an impasse. So, we need another plan."

"Haven't we kind of waited a little too long for that?"

She shrugged. "There's got to be another way."

Trevor turned away but saw a blur of motion in his side view mirror. When he gazed up at it he saw the grill of a black SUV nudge closer to his bumper. "Well," he said, "I think someone just might have made up our mind for us."

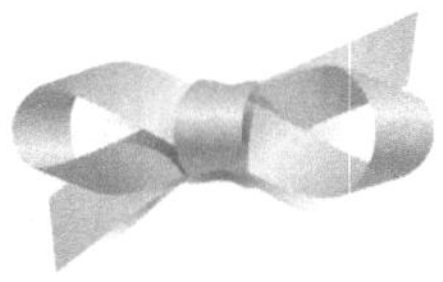

EIGHTEEN

A pair of large men in suitably dark blazers and mirrored shades manhandled Trevor and Aria, roughly pushing them inside the SUV while keeping their pistols aimed chest high. They said very little as they went about this process, which had the efficiency and coordination of professionals. In less than ten seconds they had removed them both from the car, deposited them into the SUV and were driving up toward the last ridge at a crawl.

Coming over the rise, Aria caught her first glimpse of the rendezvous point, though she strained to see any sign of her brother. She had to hand it to Mabry, especially after the fiasco at the Golden Phoenix Chinese restaurant: A covered bridge was the perfect meeting place. Open on both ends, covered overhead, Mabry and his thugs would be able to clearly see anyone coming or going from a distance. Not that it was likely anyone would be along any time soon.

A worry started to creep into her mind, that Marcus wouldn't be here at all. Worse, that he'd already be dead. That Mabry and his men had already gotten all they wanted out of her brother and might have dumped his lifeless body in some barren field or in the middle of the woods. Now, Trevor and Aria would be next in line.

That particular fear of her brother's demise was quickly dispelled as she spotted him. From this vantage point his back was to her but she could make out the telltale spill of brown hair across his neck, recognized him from his posture. The distressing part was that Marcus had been bound to a chair, hands tied behind him, legs similarly restrained, duct tape wrapped tightly around his mouth. She had time to take this all in as the SUV moved forward slowly before coming to a halt a few yards in front of the covered bridge.

The men who had forced them into the SUV now manhandled them back out, nudging Aria and Trevor forward none too kindly until the ancient planks of the dilapidated bridge were groaning beneath their feet. One man stood on each side of them, the driver remaining near the front of the vehicle where he could serve as lookout.

Aria wished yet again that she was here alone. Though she drew great strength from Trevor's presence, it seemed so wrong that his life would end today with that of her and her brother's. Guiltily, she realized that he should have ever been involved in the first place. That burden of both impending grief and responsibility weighed down upon her as she stood there and stared at the back of her brother's head, Mabry moving away from the two men standing on either side of him as he casually strolled toward the new arrivals.

"I can't tell you how glad I am that you two made it," Mabry said. "And here I was thinking you were going to try something very foolish...something that would get all three of you killed."

"I told you we would come alone," Trevor said. "Here we are."

"So it seems," Mabry said. "So it seems."

There was a muffled, urgent sound coming from Marcus, who strained to free himself from his restraints. Mabry turned to look over his shoulder, a smile creeping across his face. "I believe that Marcus wants to say something. Finally! After all this time he was so hush-hush about everything, now of all times he's got something to say!"

"Tell us what you want," Aria said. "And let him go. He's no longer useful to you anymore."

Mabry chuckled. "Well, yes and no. He was a valuable commodity as a means to get you here of course, but other than that I'd have to agree with you. His usefulness has been expended."

Trevor glared at Mabry. "What is it you think we have to offer you?"

"*You,* Officer Mason, have absolutely *nothing* that I want." Mabry put his hands behind his back, gave an almost imperceptible nod to the man standing behind Trevor. "You're what's commonly referred to as a "lose end.' As such, you are a good place for us to start...the first liability that we need to take care of."

Trevor opened his mind to speak when the guard slammed the butt of his gun over his head and he slunk to his knees, eyelids fluttering, posture as that of a penitent man in prayer. Aria gasped, started toward him but was instantly restrained, the guard behind her grabbing her by the arm and twisting it backward, forcing her to remain in place. The other guard reached down, hooking his arms under Trevor's, and began to drag him back toward the SUV.

"What are you going to do with him?" Aria demanded, hot tears spilling onto her cheeks.

"Oh, we're just going to dump him some place where he won't be found for a long, long time."

Aria craned her neck to watch as the guard dragged Trevor's limp body away. The driver positioned near the front of the SUV hustled around toward the back of the vehicle, unlatching and pulling the door before helping the first man hoist Trevor's body up and inside. This task they accomplished with efficiency, and soon they were climbing up inside the vehicle. The driver managed a tight K turn and a moment later the vehicle was rolling back up toward the hill.

"Now let's get down to business," Mabry said. "Give me the flash drive."

Aria looked at him, then withdrew the flash drive from a pocket of her jeans. "I don't know what you stand to gain by having this," she said, "The information has already been transmitted and saved."

The guard stepped forward and snatched it from her hand, handing it to Mabry. Chuckling, he said: "You *thought* you had transmitted the important stuff, all those videos of our great senate leaders getting greatly overcompensated for selling their souls. But I don't care about them...didn't I already explain that to you? We're not playing for either team...we have our own agenda, keeping it simple. We're not out here trying to buy votes or political favors. The only thing we have to gain is money, pure and simple. And as I said, that measly $10000 your brother owes us? Pardon the pun, but let's just say that's water under the bridge."

At the mentioning of her brother's name, Aria glanced at Marcus worriedly. She could not read his expressions as he was in profile, but his silence spoke volumes about their shared defeat and distress. Angrily, she shot a glance back at Mabry, who was staring at her with a grin frozen on his face.

"Now," Mabry said, "if you can excuse me for a moment I'm going to just take a minute to double check that this little device here has the information on it that is of such great value to us. I'll be back shortly."

Aria stood there in the cold, hugging herself. The guard was staring at her, expressionless and in a way that was beyond unnerving. Marcus was no longer struggling, seemingly resigned to his fate, his head lolled to one side as if he had lost the strength to keep it propped up. She turned to glance over her shoulder, but of course the van was gone. Feeling utterly alone and helpless, she couldn't quite bring herself to think about what might be happening to Trevor, though the guilt nagged at her like a pestering fly.

God...please, somehow, help all this to turn out for the good. Even if you have to let them take me, I pray that you'll spare Marcus and Trevor. Please, Lord...

Mabry returned a minute or two after he had left, each step causing the frail boards of the old, covered bridge to creak and moan. Aria had a distant thought that he must have been checking the flash drive on a laptop in the other vehicle. She could see it parked there on the other end, just a few feet beyond the bridge itself.

As he approached, she was reminded of all the times as a kid that she and Marcus had explored this bridge. They would venture out to the bridge on their bikes and crawl around on the stanchions, riding through the tunnel like runaway bank robbers, marveling over the crackling of the wood beneath their treads, admiring the way the light from the river glistened through the cracks, and breathing in the pleasing aromas of ancient wood, crabgrass, and the nearby farm. Even way back then the county had long since put the bridge of out commission—at least in regard to vehicle crossings, another reason why Mabry and his goons could figure on being left relatively alone on this desolate road. Squinting past Mabry, she saw that he and the others had ripped the planks off of the other side of the bridge, apparently tossing them carelessly aside.

Misreading her thoughts, Mabry snickered: "Pretty good plan, don't you think? There's a motorboat tied up beneath the bridge. Once we're done dealing with you and your brother we will make our escape by way of the river. As providence would have it, it's thawed enough now that we can traverse it, otherwise we'd have to take our chances on back roads and something tells me that would have been a lost cause. After all, all that money would be useless if we were captured by the Feds, wouldn't it?"

Aria knew that the only thing keeping her brother and her from being killed was time. *Keep him talking, appeal to his pride. Don't men like him just love sharing how superior they are to the common, law-abiding citizen? If you can just keep yourself alive for a little while longer—and keep Marcus alive in the process—then maybe the Feds will get here and take care of the rest.*

It might not be a great plan, but it was the only one she could conjure up under the circumstances. She leveled her gaze at Mabry, and asked softly: "So...do you care to share what is so important that you'd kill for that flash drive? That you'd ransack my house and invade my life?"

Mabry weighed this for a moment. "I suppose I can satisfy a little of your curiosity, now that I've verified that I've got what I need. But don't think I'm going to fall into the trap of that tired old trope that you see in so many movies where I just reveal all the intricacies of our well thought out plan and then the good guys come swooping in just in time to save the day. We're going to wrap this up quickly and we're gone."

"You're going to kill us? Both of us...right here, in cold blood?"

"When you put it like that it sounds so cruel," Mabry said. "So heartless and mean." He spread his hands. "All this is just business, sweetheart."

"Just let Marcus go, then. Take me if you want but let my brother go."

Mabry cocked his head, this offer of self-sacrifice seemingly foreign to his understanding, giving her a peculiar look as if a colorful bird had just landed on her head and begun reciting the Pledge of Allegiance. "How...how am I supposed to do that when he not only betrayed me but knows enough so that he could lead the authorities to me?"

"I don't know," Aria said. "Just...can't you show a little mercy? Do you see how scared he is? He was so frightened he tried to run from you guys...what makes you think he's going to turn around and give you up or testify or whatever it is you think he might do? He's going to *run* from this. That's what he always does."

She regretted saying that last even as the words left her mouth. Marcus shrunk back as if slapped. Worse still, Mabry had taken notice and now a wider grin was spreading across his face. "Family drama," he said. "Interesting. You two must have had a troubled relationship growing up."

"That's none of your business," Aria said. She felt herself blushing, and hugged herself tighter, averting her eyes from Mabry, who began to chuckle. Worse than that, she felt like she'd lost a little control over herself.

"Well," he said, "as interesting as it would be to delve into all the trauma and unspoken words and regrets that you two siblings have shared over your lifetimes, I'm afraid I have to duck out. Time is quickly slipping away."

Aria stepped forward and immediately realized too late that it might have been a big mistake...her last, even. The guard standing by Mabry took a step toward her as well, withdrawing a gun and pointing it at her. Aria froze, closing her eyes, thinking that this really might be it. That the end had come and whatever precious seconds she had left might have just been sacrificed.

"Now," Mabry said. "I will give you one last choice."

She finally pried her eyes open, looked at him.

He aimed his gun at her head, then slid it toward Marcus, who cowered in the chair. "Who's going first? You, or your brother? I'll let you make the decision."

Aria opened her mouth to speak, the tears—more frustration than anything else—springing to her eyes already. *Me...shoot me and let him go,* she was going to say. It had never been a thought—not so much as a hesitation. Even after all this time, all the arguments and regrets and words left unspoken, she loved her brother just as deeply as ever and would give anything—even her own life—to save him.

Before she could get the words out she heard the crunch of tires on snow. Mabry's gaze shifted from her to something beyond the bridge. To whoever was coming. At the same time, his smile faltered and she saw the gun drift down a few inches, still aimed somewhere between her and Marcus. There was a look of confusion on his face, which quickly melted into anger.

"What can it possibly be now?" He grumbled under his breath, just loud enough for Aria to hear.

Aria turned slowly, not wanting to draw Mabry's attention to her again. She caught a glimpse of the SUV rolling forward and her heart sunk. Mabry's men were back already, which meant they had done the grisly deed. They had killed Trevor.

Her breath hitched, she felt water filling her eyes. She didn't want to cry—not in front of this man. She held back her sorrow like a great mass of water behind a dam. But something else gave her pause—the sound of Mabry's voice when he had spoken, matched with the expression on her face.

Something was off, someone had changed the plan. *He's wondering why they're back so quickly. They hadn't even been gone for five minutes.*

Confused, she turned and looked at the SUV. Both men were sitting in the front seats, staring out at them blankly from behind their sunglasses. Their faces were emotionless...the blank visage of cold-hearted killers.

Mabry remained frozen in place, gun raised around waist level, his attention on the vehicle. It was rolling to a stop, the engine idling. Something palpable had shifted in the atmosphere—it was unmistakable to Aria that something wasn't right. If she couldn't have told that by the confusion that was slowly spreading across Mabry's face she would have been able to by the ominous feeling that hung in the air.

What in the world...

NINETEEN

Both the guard behind the wheel and his companion in the passenger seat ducked slowly below the dashboard, even as the SUV began rolling forward, the thin scrim of ice and snow crunching beneath the tires. Reflexively, Aria rolled to the left, splinters of wood digging into the palms of her hands as she began to crawl toward her brother.

Behind her, the guard had temporarily forgotten about her, more in tune at that moment to the approaching SUV, his expression mirroring Mabry's own confusion and uncertainty. He held the gun pointed at the SUV but was frozen in indecision. Almost helplessly, he looked toward Mabry who glared back at him and screamed: "Shoot them!"

Turning, the guard brought the gun around in a slow, unsteady arc as the SUV advanced toward them. He fired a single shot, which ricocheted off the hood of the SUV. Undaunted, the vehicle kept coming at a leisurely—but deadly—pace, relentlessly grinding through the mud and snow and crunching ice.

Mabry also reacted right away, stepping forward as he lowered the gun and aimed it directly at the SUV like a hunter standing in the path of a lumbering bear. He had not yet fired though, choosing instead to rage against the vehicle's unseen drivers. "Stop!" He yelled, his voice echoing like thunder through the clouds as his voice reverberated through the covered bridge. "I order you to stop! What are you doing? I said *STOP!*" His face had turned beet red and his hands were shaking.

Suddenly, the guard fired off two more shots in rapid succession, one popping a hole high on the windshield and the other shattering the driver's side headlight. Mabry also fired, four times. He shouted again for the driver to stop but held his ground, his own weapon smoking in his outstretched and trembling hand.

Aria kept moving forward, crawling across the bridge on her hands and knees. Below her, the gaps between the boards beneath her feet gave her a fragmented view of the silver ribbon of the gently flowing river, the surface sparkling like scattered diamonds. Something shuddered, the sensation violent enough to cause her to lay down flat on the boards. Behind them, the SUV had reached the bridge and did not hesitate at the threshold as the tires rolled over the first board.

Creeeeeeeak!

Trembling—either from the shuddering framework of the bridge itself or the icy grip of fear that had squeezed her in its fist—Aria forced herself from off the floor and back on her hands and knees, creeping toward Marcus.

A few feet away, both Mabry and the guard paid no attention to their prisoners. As the SUV came into contact with him, the guard stepped aside almost casually, firing three more shots directly through the passenger window at unseen occupants as the vehicle passed by. Mabry remained center forward, less than ten feet from the vehicle's hood, but keeping pace with it as he backpedaled slowly. The muzzle of his gun was still pointed at the SUV but for now he was simply glaring down the barrel in defiance.

As the tires began to roll onto the bridge and the delicate boards, Aria caught a glimpse of motion in her peripheral vision and turned toward the driver's side of the SUV in time to see Trevor slipping down from the back seat. Crouching on the ground he pressed the driver's door gingerly closed until it latched, then inched his way forward, using the SUV as a shield.

Aria's mind was spinning, trying to sort out everything. *How did he—* Immediately, the question answered itself as she began to put it all together. Somehow, Trevor had revived himself, overtaken the men, and knocked them out of commission. Then he'd propped them up like decoys in their respective seats and shifted the gear into neutral. With the downward grade he only had to let momentum do the rest of the work.

Mabry spotted Trevor a moment later and jerked his head in that direction, wheeling around a moment later as he fired off a shot that went wide.

Ducking out of reflex, Trevor hunkered down and aimed his own weapon—no doubt purloined from one of the incapacitated guards—firing back. Mabry ducked, hobbling toward the other side of the van for cover.

Still unmindful of her, Aria's guard had joined Mabry to address the new threat. He backed up a few steps while aiming his gun and fired when Trevor popped back into sight. But Trevor was darting quickly forward, diving toward the ground in a roll. The bullet wasn't even close and as Trevor came out of the roll he was in a squatting shooter's stance, gun aimed directly at the guard. He squeezed off a single shot.

The guard cried out, grabbing his arm just above the left bicep before turning and lurching away from the SUV. Crossing through the covered bridge, he broke into a hobbling run as he headed for Mabry's vehicle, parked on the other end.

"Hey!" Mabry yelled at his back. "Where are you going? Get over here, now!"

It was a lost cause. The guard wasn't even looking back as he neared the other end of the bridge.

In all the commotion, Aria had remained unnoticed, so she kept moving forward, crawling quickly toward her brother. She felt the earthquake tremble of the bridge's planks and support and paused a moment, heart beating as she braced herself. *It's all going to come down around us,* she thought. *If we don't get off this bridge soon, we might all die in a heap of old boards.*

As if sensing the same thing, Marcus strained against his restraints, struggled to cry out through the tape that covered his mouth. Turned away from her, he hadn't yet caught a glimpse of Aria but he was jerking around so violently that he was about to overturn the chair.

Aria was momentarily frozen in place; the whole bridge seeming to sway and tremble around her. Finally, she chanced a look over her shoulder.

The SUV was now completely on the bridge, its great weight causing the whole bridge to shift dangerously, swaying slightly side to side. The boards groaned and moaned and snapped with the sound of an old man stretching on a rocking chair. There was a deafening snap as one of the boards broke in half, leaving a foot-wide gap in the bridge where the tire had passed. The SUV was gliding slowly across the bridge on a one-way mission to commit massive destruction.

...and to provide a distraction.

Now! Aria told herself. *Move, now before it's too late and the whole bridge collapses.*

But it was worse than that, she quickly reminded herself. If the SUV kept going and did indeed rattle the ancient structure apart, they would all be sent plunging into the icy river together. She had to get herself and Marcus out of there before it happened.

Mabry stubbornly held his ground, standing now to let the SUV pass in front of him while aiming over the hood to take a shot at one of them. Aria grabbed the back of Marcus' chair and pulled him backward just in time. The gunshot echoed through the air, but it appeared for now that she and Marcus had remained unharmed.

The back of the chair was against the bridge, with Marcus staring up at the top. Into the eaves where they had once found an owl's nest on a late afternoon in July as children exploring the bridge's many nooks and crannies. Aria remembered rushing out of there, fearful that mama owl might come back and claw their faces to shreds.

Trevor was crouched over, drawing near to Aria and Marcus even as his attention remained focused on Mabry. He fired a shot but it hit the driver's side window, sending a spider web network of cracks across the surface. The bad news was now there was an obstruction from which Mabry could hide from them. But the good news was that the same went for the little trio on the other side.

The crunch and crackling of wood sounded like gunshots reverberating in the enclosure. Pieces of wood were splitting, jutting up from the floor of the bridge like spears. The bridge itself swayed back and forth, and all of them knew intuitively that it would eventually swing so wide to one side that it wouldn't come back...it'd keep going and they would all go with it.

...And still the SUV came.

From his moving barricade Mabry began to fire his gun blindly, first snapping off two shots that punched through both the passenger and driver windows and then with a third that went through unhindered, though the shot was high and wide and hit nothing of consequence. At the same time, he kept pace with the SUV's advance, backing up step after step and keeping a good ten-foot space between him and the others.

Aria's guard had disappeared, but not before she'd caught a glimpse of him on the other side of the bridge, shimmying down the shoulder toward the river. *If Mabry doesn't act quickly his mode of escape is going to be long gone. Or maybe the guy will just keep running across the snowy fields.*

Trevor was now yelling above the cacophony of splintering boards, waving for her to get going, to get off the bridge. It did sound like Armageddon inside the old bridge, but Aria wouldn't leave until she had freed her brother...there was no way she was going to leave him there. Bound to the chair, he would be crushed by the bridge, drowned in the river, or suffer hypothermia. None of those eventualities sounded any better than the other.

As Trevor moved away from them toward the SUV She got her fingers on the ropes, started fumbling for the restraints that kept her brother's hands bound. Marcus struggled to speak, his muffled voice frantic, his eyes wide with terror. But that would have to wait. First, she wanted to get his hands free and then his legs. Better that he could have mobility than the ability to speak, especially with the thought of the bridge crashing down. *Trevor's plan was a brilliant one but won't be worth much if we don't get out of here alive.*

Furiously, she began to unwind the cords around Marcus' hands. Her hands trembling, it proved a cumbersome task, but she encouraged herself by realizing she was making slow but steady progress getting them unwound. Finally, his hands free, Marcus reached up and ripped off the rag around his mouth. "We gotta hurry, Aria!" He sputtered. "The bridge..."

"I know, I know!" Aria replied, reaching for the restraints around her brother's feet even as he attempted to help with the task. Something caught her attention and she turned in time to see Mabry coming toward them around the front of the SUV, swinging his gun around. Her eyes grew wide when she saw that Trevor hadn't seen the other man yet was right in the line of fire.

"Trevor!" She screamed.

Too late. The gun barked in Mabry's hand and Trevor jerked away like he had touched a live wire. His body was flung like an old coat across the bridge and he landed on his back on the rough wood, the gun coming loose from his grip. Motionless, he stared up at the roof of the bridge like Marcus had just a moment before.

Mabry staggered forward, careful to avoid the turning wheels, breathing in shallow, ragged gasps. The gun was in his hand and he looked down at Aria and Marcus with an expression of vehement rage. He lowered the gun.

A rifle crack boomed through the bridge as one of the central girders beneath the bridge suddenly gave way. The bridge rocked, throwing Mabry backwards before he could get off a shot. Stumbling, he collided with the SUV and then slunk to the ground, a look of confusion seizing his expression. Behind him, the SUV shuddered, lurched, began to slide down into the disintegrating supports, the path having disappeared in front of it.

There was an enormous crunching sound, and one of the supports above cracked in two like a broken rib, slid down and crashed through the bridge.

Hurriedly, Aria began to unwind the restraints around her brother's legs. His eyes were wide with fright as they felt the whole bridge—from tip to tip—lean precariously to the left. The weight of the SUV was bringing it under, inexorably causing it to slide beneath the supports and seeming to take the bridge with it. Aria's fingers moved nimbly as she focused on the task at hand. A moment later and Marcus was freed.

A few feet away Trevor had regained consciousness and was slowly moving forward, one hand clutching his bloody bicep. Though his face was twisted in pain, he focused his eyes intensely on the SUV in front of him. There was a look of absolute determination on his face, his jaw clenched and his eyes narrowed. *Do or die, he's gonna make this happen,* Aria thought, her heart lurching in her chest. *Please, God, help him!*

Mabry was on his hands and knees, stunned, searching for his lost weapon. Then he spotted it there almost equidistant between he and Trevor.

The pair locked eyes and Mabry's face pinched into what looked to Aria something like that of an angry dog. Trevor's eyes narrowed, lips pressed into a thin, determined line. Simultaneously, the two men dove toward the gun, their hands outstretched.

At that very moment the SUV lost its battle, crashing through the boards before disappearing into empty space.

The boards folded inward in the wake of the vehicle's passing, the tops popping free from their place and sending nails singing overhead. Mabry screamed—more out of panic than pain, Aria figured—and fell back again to his knees, holding onto the plank beneath him like a surfer climbing back up on his board after being attacked by a shark. Mabry's face was bleached white, the panic draining all the blood out. He clung to the board even as he began to slide backward toward the void.

Far below, the SUV slammed through the boat like a hammer into a cardboard box. There was a mighty crackling splash as the SUV found the half-frozen river and smashed through the brittle surface. The remainder of the bridge that remained standing issued a piercing complaint.

Trevor stared at the gun. He had closed much of the distance when the floor of the bridge had suddenly dropped away and engulfed the SUV. Now his gaze ticked back and forth between it and Mabry, who was crying out in fear: "Please-oh-please-oh-please! SAVE ME!"

Resigned to his decision, Trevor rushed toward the fallen man, diving onto the ground and reaching for him just as Mabry lost his grip and began to slide backward toward the gaping hole in the bridge.

There was another long and agonizing groan as the bridge strained against itself like a dying beast. Moorings were snapping lose, pieces of metal flying off like shrapnel, wood cracking and splitting and breaking in two all around them.

Finally freed, Marcus shot out of the chair, toppling it over, then stumbled as he tried to find the strength in his legs. He crawled toward Trevor, who had his hands locked around Mabry's wrist and was holding on for dear life. Still, both men were drifting slowly backward, as if Mabry had not fallen toward a hole in the bridge but into quicksand.

Already on her hands and knees, Aria reached for Marcus as he tumbled again to the floor of the lurching bridge. Terrified, she clambered for him. The whole bridge was coming apart, the fragile, age-worn wood unable to take the mortal wound that the SUV had left in its heart. He wouldn't be thwarted, dead set on coming to Trevor's aid...to rescue the man that had done all he could to kill them.

Aria reacted without thinking, rushing after him toward the jagged hole. Mabry was sliding slowly into the gap, his face a mask of horror and desperation. Trevor fought to hang on but it looked like his other hand was failing him as it scrabbled for purchase but found only the smooth sides of the ancient boards.

In desperation he reached out for a hold—anything—but could not find anything in his blind search. This was it, the final moment: He would need to let go of Mabry, let the man plunge to his fate or he would join him. Then, suddenly, a hand shot out and grabbed him around the forearm, another soon joining the first to hold tight to the back of his shirt. Trevor turned to see Marcus grinning down at him.

"Hang in there," Marcus said. "We've got you."

Straining, the cords of his neck standing out on his neck, Trevor fought to hold onto Mabry with one hand. Aria had reached her brother's side now, sliding onto her stomach as she reached out and grabbed Mabry's other leg. She pulled and pulled but was unable to do much to help.

Marcus clenched his jaw and strained back as he tried to pull Trevor to safety. Aria lugged on Mabry's leg, the other man's hand fluttering up to grab hold of a nearby board. Just past him she could see the river and the crushed boat, the pile of debris that had once been part of the bridge's superstructure. The current, running at a lazy, meandering pace, seemed like a mile below their feet.

"Hang on!" She yelled at the top of her voice, though she wasn't exactly sure who she was directing the words to at that moment. Any of them. All of them.

Together, and with agonizingly slow progress, the three of them were able to begin to leverage the advantage, slowly bringing Mabry back from the edge. Below them, Mabry's face was frozen in fright, the white of the snowy banks and the silver- blue of the river a dramatic backdrop to the ordeal. Mabry held tight to the board, tried to do what he could to pull himself out.

Slowly, they began to hoist him upward. Aria could feel every muscle screaming against the effort, and she figured that the two men were suffering the same. Not a single one of them could have accomplished the task themselves—they probably couldn't even have managed it with just two—but in a concerted effort the little band was making progress.

"Just...stay calm," Trevor gasped. Shifting his position around, he found a better angle and with Marcus' help was able to begin dragging Mabry forward. Now he had two hands free to try and work Mabry back up through the aperture and onto the crumbling bridge.

Finally, they rolled Mabry back onto the bridge and onto his back. On shaking feet, Trevor managed to stand, stepping over and snatching up the gun, which he pointed at Mabry just in case the other man decided to try something.

"The guard," Aria said, gesturing toward the other end of the bridge. "There's still one more." Shivering, she pointed toward the field. "He's down there."

Trevor nodded, unconcerned. "In all the commotion—and after getting shot—he took off, running across that field. He won't get far. I called the cavalry before driving the SUV back down to the bridge. They should be arriving here at any moment."

"You really must have been certain that maneuver would have worked, huh?" She asked.

"Not really," he shrugged. "But it was the only thing I could come up with, and at that it was our last chance. When you only have one option, you take it."

"Well," Marcus chimed in, standing bent over with his hands on his knees as he tried to catch his breath. "It worked. That's the main thing."

On all fours, Mabry was gasping for breath, a landed fish on the shore. Sputtering, he said: "I...I coulda died...you...you saved me. W-W-Why would you do that?"

"Two reasons I can think of," Trevor said. "First, because we're not like you. Second, because you need to be made to answer for your crimes."

Mabry turned away, bringing both of his trembling hands up to cradle his head. The bridge, having dislodged the heavy SUV through its midsection, was swaying gently now, returning to its tremulous resting position. Though it couldn't have suffered much more after the last few minutes, it seemed to be steadying now. If they took it slowly, they would make it off the rickety old thing.

Mabry led the way, hands over his head, Trevor with the gun aimed at the middle of his back. They were heading toward Mabry's own vehicle. Behind him, Aria threw her arm around Marcus and when he looked at her he offered a relieved but nervous smile.

Only then did they hear the sirens rising in the distance.

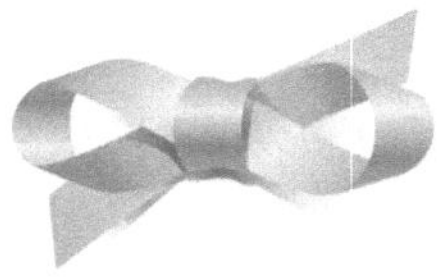

TWENTY

The cavalry did indeed arrive, descending upon the broken bridge like wasps, red and blue lights spinning overhead. Several cruisers closed off either end of the bridge before disgorging a dozen state troopers. A helicopter buzzed overhead, flying low as it passed the bridge and then swooped out over the snowy field beyond. The fleeing guard, quickly drained of energy and shivering uncontrollably as he trudged through the waist-high mixture of slush and snow, was found less than a quarter mile away.

Aria and Trevor huddled together on the trunk of his patrol car, watching the scene being processed, a heavy gray blanket—courtesy of the fire department—flung over each of their shoulders. They sat numbly, saying nothing as their exhausted bodies tried to recover. Marcus had already been escorted to a large van and was being interrogated by the authorities. Aria knew better than to think she wouldn't have to endure her own rounds of probing questions when the time came, but right now she was enjoying her little reprieve.

Vincent Mabry was escorted off the bridge in handcuffs and deposited into a waiting squad car. As he was being arrested and searched, the flash drive was found on his person and placed in an evidence bag. FBI agents—real ones, not imposters—were swarming over his vehicle like ants on a peanut butter and jelly sandwich, and Aria spotted a laptop being sequestered away by a man in a black suit with gloves on his hands. Mabry sat in gloomy silence, staring despondently over the broken bridge and his own shattered agenda, one which left around a dozen bodies in his wake.

As if reading her thoughts, another agent approached her and said: "You both did a great job. The contents of the flash drive will reveal banking account information. Though it's been established that there were bribes given to the senators for ensuring a certain vote on a military appropriations bill, Mabry and his thugs were the ones who were really going to make out, at least monetarily. We have the evidence to bring all of the guilty participants down."

Trevor glanced at him. "Any idea how much money was at stake?"

"To the tune of a quarter billion, give or take," he said. "That's my understanding at least at this preliminary stage of the investigation."

Trevor whistled, turning to Aria. "The fact that Marcus knew that, let alone having the flash drive with the account information on it was more than enough to get him killed."

"That's why he wanted to keep moving," Aria observed. "Coming back here to Anderson's Crossroads was a bad idea but he was desperate. I don't think he was really thinking through the repercussions of his actions at the time—putting so many people at risk."

"All that money. Mabry basically shrugged off the ten thousand Marcus owed him," Trevor mused. "That's a drop in the bucket to what they stood to make once they were able to get their hands on the flash drive."

"Yep," Aria said, running her fingers through her hair. "Guess they're going to want to have a long conversation with us about all this before it's all said and done."

About an hour after he'd gone into the van, Marcus emerged, spotted them amidst the bustle and walked over, looking suitably chagrined. "Well," he said, "that wasn't exactly what I'd call fun."

"Well, I hate to be the bearer of bad news," Trevor said, "but all that 'fun' is just beginning. There's a bright side, though. If you just stick to the facts I'm sure you'll come through it relatively unscathed. Tell them how you knew you were in deep, deep danger...how you were running scared."

"*Scared* is the right word," Marcus admitted. "I was fleeing for fear of my life. I'm just...I'm sorry I got you involved, Sis."

Aria crossed her arms over her chest as she watched the squad car in which one Vincent Mabry was seated begin to pull away. "I'm just glad that you're safe," she said. "That *all* of us are." She smiled up at Trevor before taking his hand in her own.

"If it makes you feel any better, there's going to be a lot of questions for all of us," Trevor told Marcus. "But it'll all work out in the end. Just tell them the truth...everything you know."

Marcus nodded. "Yeah. I will. No matter what happens, I'm...I'm tired of running."

They both knew what he meant and they nodded reassuringly. Trevor pulled Aria closer and she tucked her head under his chin. For the first time in several days, she was finally beginning to feel safe.

The interrogation process was exhausting, as the authorities tried to unravel all the threads that had gotten a whole FBI team and most of a small town's police force killed.

Everyone operated under the unspoken assumption that this was only the beginning...that the tendrils of what had happened would prove to reach very, very deep. Just *how* far had yet to be determined, but Trevor and Aria knew that it was a case for others besides themselves to figure out. And that suited them just fine.

By the time the *real* FBI was done with them it was nearing dusk, and Aria and Trevor were both starving to death. He gave her a wicked glance and suggested: "Chinese?"

Aria groaned. "Usually that'd be an immediate 'yes,' but not after the events at the Golden Phoenix. Maybe some other time. Plus, we need to grab something quick."

"Oh?" Trevor asked, his eyebrows knitting together. "What's the rush?"

She gave him a look of mock irritation. "Um...our date. Remember?"

Trevor's eyebrows lifted. "The Christmas program!"

Aria nodded, smiling. "There for a while I was afraid we might miss it."

"I wouldn't miss it for the world...or even a dangerous shoot out with bad guys on a dilapidated bridge." Trevor turned Aria around until she was facing him. "I'm awfully proud of you, lady."

"For what?"

"Are you kidding? Where should I start? For being so brave, how about that?"

She grinned mischievously. "I guess I did kinda save you back there on the bridge."

"Well, now let's not get carried away," he said.

"No," she said, leaning toward him. "Let's..."

They kissed, and as Aria closed her eyes she felt all her cares melting away, at least for the time being. Lost in this tender embrace, she had escaped for a moment into another life where the future looked as bright as a cloudless summer day. Where there were no closed-door meetings with sweaty men in suits and ties, no courtrooms or reporters or worries about someone trying to come back to exact vengeance. No gunfire in a library or shooting at a police department. No break-ins and vandalism and mysterious figures lurking around every corner. Just her and this man who had become suddenly such an important part of her life. She wished she could hold onto the moment forever.

As they slowly pulled apart, she could see an almost angelic glow on Trevor's face. He shook his head slowly. "You really are amazing. I just don't know why I waited so long to really try to get to know you. I guess I was just intimidated. Thought you were...I don't know, somehow unreachable."

Aria smirked, shaking her head. "You sound pathetic."

Trevor's eyes widened in surprise. "Really? I..."

"I'm just kidding," she said quickly, laughing. "You are very sweet and super cute. I also wonder why it took you so long."

"Well, it was worth the wait," Trevor said. "Well worth it, in fact."

"Agreed," Aria said. She took his hands again and gave them a squeeze. "But one thing I can't wait on much longer is dinner."

Dinner ended up being a drive through at a fast-food hamburger joint. Not exactly as Aria had envisioned their first dinner date, but she was grateful just the same. They wolfed it down on their way to church and managed to arrive with the others who had enjoyed just a more traditional Christmas Eve day, the kind without all the gunfire and imminent death.

Aria took a deep breath. "We really did make it," she said.

Trevor nodded proudly. "We did. But this program better be good, the way you've been selling it."

She gave him a mock angry glance and then laughed. "It might not be very good, but it will be perfectly *nice*. And you better be also. These are my people in there, you know."

"Yes ma'am."

Opening the door, she paused to look back at him one more time. "I really am happy you're here with me," she said. "Not to mention that you probably saved both me and my brother's life."

"Just doin' my duty, ma'am." He said with the tip of an imaginary hat. "But, seriously, it was all worth it just so that I could get to know Miss Aria Chambers a little better. I hope that this is just the first of many mediocre Christmas Eve programs to come."

She considered that for a moment. "Me too."

Christmas Day
TWENTY-ONE

Aria busily flitted around her home as she finished preparations for the Christmas get together. She checked her watch and saw that it was nearing ten o'clock, which meant folks were going to be arriving soon. She looked over the dining room table one more time, making sure her mental calculations reconciled with the place settings on the table. Satisfied, she returned to the stove to check on the pork loin.

After the Christmas program Trevor had brought her home and then graciously helped her clean up the debris left after Mabry's men had ransacked the place. The front door was still broken but Trevor had screwed it shut, promising to replace the door when businesses reopened tomorrow. Thankfully, the kitchen door would serve as a good entrance and exit for her guests.

Aria *had* managed to find a drug store near the Interstate that was open on Christmas day and had bought the items missing from her pantry that would make a Christmas meal complete. Now she thought that she might have everything in order.

Marcus was the first to arrive. He would be remaining in Anderson's Crossing for a few days though both of them knew that he would be busy dealing with the big case. As far as that went, the whole event was all that was playing on the big news stations: CNN, MSNBC, and FOX were airing footage of the senators that had gotten arrested for their involvement that was quickly being dubbed THE CHRISTMAS CONSPIRACY due to the fact that things all were coming to a head over the past several days. Several of the conspirators had been tracked down, some having been picked up at airports trying to slip out of the country.

There was also coverage of Vincent Mabry and his coordination of the assassination of a six-member FBI team. It had already been established that Mabry had heartlessly orchestrated the gunning down of the team simply to provide cover for his own attempt to clean up the quickly disintegrating plot. Following that had been the assault on the Anderson's Crossing police office. Aria feared the fallout of that assault, and what it would mean for both Trevor and his family as they tried to navigate the grief that came with losing so many coworkers and friends. She figured that the full weight of it hadn't yet settled over him.

"Hey, Sis," Marcus said, giving her the briefest of hugs. "You got a minute?"

Aria glanced at the clock mounted near the Christmas tree in the living room. "Of course."

He led her out onto the kitchen porch. Leaning against the railing, he looked out over the front yard to the road, but his thoughts were elsewhere. On the future, Aria figured.

"Look," he said. "I want to say sorry again, one more time. I—"

"Marcus...you don't have to keep apologizing. It's over now."

He sighed. "Mostly, I guess. I'm not sure what's coming next for me. I might be going to jail though...it's definitely a possibility. I'll find out soon enough. But I need you to know something before we get too far apart again."

Aria looked at him, feeling something both strange and familiar bubbling up inside. Something akin to nostalgia, she supposed, but much deeper than that. It was the colliding of a lifetime of memories that she had shared with him coming tumbling through her mind and the thought that everything from here on out was going to change.

"Whatever happens," Marcus said, "I need you to know that I haven't been doing anything. Drugs, I mean. I've been going to the meetings, trying to walk the straight and narrow. I hesitate to say I'm clean because that's when it all seems to fall apart. Once an addict, always an addict, right?"

"I don't believe that," Aria said. "I do believe in you, though."

He smiled that cocky smile of his but she saw something register in his eyes. That her words had immediately touched him. "Thanks," he said. "But I have been clean for over a year now. All that trouble with the senators and these people trying to kill us. That's a whole different issue. Trouble, yeah, but it had nothing to do with drugs.

"I was working for these people as a driver...mainly bringing people from one place to the other. Sometimes I had packages but I swear I thought it was above board. These people had *offices,* for goodness' sake. We weren't doing business behind a dumpster or in the back room of a bar."

"All right," Aria said.

"I did start to figure out that there was some shadiness to what I was doing, but these suits are always doing shady things, right? Real estate stuff, insider trading, other scams. I figured that I could keep my hands clean and look the other way. After a while it was at a point where I *couldn't* get out. That they'd kill me if I tried. And when I tried to leave, that's just what happened."

"You figured out that there were bribes being paid to senators?"

Marcus offered a mirthless chuckle. "Who keeps up with the names of senators or what they look like? I'll tell you one person who doesn't: Me. I only found out when someone started talking about it. Then I was stuck. I had to keep going. Aria...you gotta understand something: I risked my life to get away from these people, and when I knew that they had all kinds of connections and ways to track me down."

"What happened next?" Aria asked.

"That's when I came down here," Marcus said, shame causing him to avert his gaze. "But I decided to get a little revenge—call it 'justice,' actually—by taking the flash drive with all the evidence on it. That was one thing—having leverage. What I didn't realize was that I also had the routing numbers for all the money that Mabry and the people he was working with were after."

Aria looked past Marcus to the road, which was empty. "Do you think..."

Marcus glanced at her, then followed her gaze, reading her thoughts. "No one's coming after us now. Just the real Feds, wanting their pound of flesh, especially with what happened to their field team."

Aria nodded silently. She'd seen coverage that morning of the discovery of the murdered FBI team on a dead-end road in the woods just outside of North Platte. She was afraid that Marcus could be right about one thing in particular: That the Feds' demand for justice might catch him up in the fallout. She prayed that it wouldn't come to that. Marcus was assisting and cooperating and doing all he could to bring the case to a resolution and to keep himself in their good graces. As he inferred, they'd have to wait and see.

Marcus had stopped talking and was now just staring at the horizon. Aria sensed he was still struggling with something. Finally, he said: "You said you believe in me?"

"Yes."

"That's the most important thing to me right now," he said. "That you believe in me. Mom and Dad probably won't ever, but—"

"Never say 'never,'" Aria said, putting her arm around his shoulder. "Give them a chance. Wait for the air to clear. Marcus...you're their son, and they miss you."

He thought about that and then just nodded. "I suppose, but I'm not ready to face them just yet."

"Where will you go?" Aria asked.

Marcus scratched his chin. "I have some friends that I'm going to stay with for Christmas and maybe a few days after that. Then...well, then I'll figure it out."

"Okay," Aria said. "Just make sure and take care of yourself and don't flake out on this whole case. It's serious."

"I know."

"I love you, Marcus."

He turned and looked at her, his eyes misty. "I love you, too."

Trevor arrived with his great grandmother Olivia just after ten. After retrieving her from the Dillahunts' he had kept her in her own house for the night. Edward had stayed on as well. Since he didn't have any family in the area he accepted the invitation to Aria's with barely contained enthusiasm.

When the three of them arrived, Aria gave the caretaker a warm hug at the door and welcomed him in as part of their patchwork family. Trevor followed, wheeling Olivia in her chair and finding her a spot relatively close to the Christmas tree (at her request).

Sunday School teacher Ralph Schaeffer and his wife arrived shortly after eleven, thankful for having been invited. The older couple had no family of their own around other than that of their congregation. Eva had prepared her (locally) famous strawberry cheesecake for the occasion. A couple of other friends from church had made it, toting gifts and casserole dishes as they came through the kitchen door.

Aria wondered to herself when the last time was that she had any kind of group over that she might consider family. She wistfully considered that she had been in her little shell for long enough. That it was time to stretch her wings and see more of the world. To finally escape from her own cycle of grief. She wished that her parents had been able to make it today, but she was grateful for those who were in attendance. It would doubtlessly prove to be a special day. She was mentally making plans to visit them in Arizona before the weather down there got too hot.

Marcus left after dinner, shouldering his backpack like he was shrugging into the weight of the world and giving her a kiss on the cheek. He waved to the rest of the folks still in attendance before making his way to the kitchen and out the door. Before he left he gave Aria a big hug and swore that he'd be doing a better job staying in touch. An ancient-looking Chevy Citation pulled up to the end of the driveway. With his backpack over his shoulder, Marcus made his way down the driveway, not pausing to look back. Aria watched him go and waved to the car as it pulled off.

At some point, long after whatever gifts had been exchanged were opened and everybody was full of pork loin, scalloped potatoes, green beans, yeast rolls and a variety of delicious pies, Trevor found her in the kitchen. He stood across from her for a moment before clearing his throat. "So," he said. "I'm about to take Grandma Olivia back to the nursing home in North Platte. She's about ready to take her afternoon siesta I think. Edward will be leaving, too."

Aria smiled at him. "I'm glad you came. And thank you for last night."

"You're welcome," he said. "Thank you for lunch today. It was absolutely wonderful. I never really know what to do on Christmas now that my family is gone or scattered across the United States."

"Yeah," Aria said, thinking of her own parents. Of Marcus, who would be flitting off somewhere soon enough, if he managed to avoid jail time. "I know what you mean. It seems like nothing lasts forever."

"Maybe so," Trevor said. "But I hope we get to see where our relationship goes. I really care about you, Aria. I think I always really have."

Aria looked away, reigning in her emotions. "For so long I thought that I wouldn't be able to care about someone again. Not like I did before. Like I had invested so much into someone and then they were just snatched away from me. It was so hard."

Trevor said nothing, just reached for her and found her hand. "We can certainly take our time. I mean if you're even interested in pursuing anything. If not, I—"

"No," Aria said, blurting it out too quickly. Blushing, she averted her eyes, measuring her words before meeting his gaze again. "What I mean is that I *am* interested, and It's past time for me to stop closing myself off, especially to someone who I think is really worth the effort."

"Okay," Trevor said uncertainly. "So maybe I can get your new door when the hardware store opens tomorrow and get that fixed up and then...dinner?"

"Dinner sounds fantastic," Aria said. "Though you certainly have no obligation to fix the door."

"It'd be my pleasure," Trevor said. "Restore some sense of normalcy for you after all the craziness that's happened this past week."

"Normal sounds good," Aria said, taking a deep breath. "And dinner with you sounds even better."

"Are you saying I'm not normal?" Trevor said, feigning offense.

"Not at all," Aria responded. "You are a very special guy, and I'm lucky that you've come into my life."

"Even under the circumstances?" He asked.

"Believe me," Aria said, "it's the one thing I *am* thankful for this week."

"Then that makes two of us," Trevor said, pulling her closer. He leaned toward her and she closed her eyes, lifting her chin so that his lips could find her own. He kissed her, delicately, slowly bringing up a hand to cradle her cheek. When they separated, they looked into each other's eyes and Aria felt her heart fluttering in her chest. Like it was a bird, soaring, finally set free from the past. She smiled up at him.

Suddenly, the sound of someone clearing their throat drew both of their attention to the unseen visitor standing in the door frame. It was Edward and Grandma Olivia. They were both staring numbly at Trevor and Aria as if they were lingering somewhere they had little interest in being. Embarrassed, Aria stepped away from Trevor, hands on her hips.

"Um," Edward said. "Just checking to see if you are ready to go."

Trevor cleared his throat. Nodded. "Yes. I'm on my way, just saying goodbye."

"Uh huh," Edward said, turning to wheel Eva back into the living room.

After they left Trevor glanced at Aria and they both laughed. He hesitated awkwardly, trying to think of something else to say, and then just raised his hand and gave a little wave. "Well, I guess I shall see you tomorrow then."

"Okay."

Trevor turned and exited the kitchen. Aria stood there, still recovering from the kiss and her awakening feelings. She glanced out the window where the sun was pouring through. It would indeed be good to get to normal, to maybe even fall in love again.

"Merry Christmas," She whispered to the empty room. Smiling, she returned to the living room and her guests.

THE END

Don't miss out!

Visit the website below and you can sign up to receive emails whenever Jimmy Gear publishes a new book. There's no charge and no obligation.

https://books2read.com/r/B-A-SCRWB-KWHNE

BOOKS 2 READ

Connecting independent readers to independent writers.

Did you love *A Christmas Conspiracy*? Then you should read *Captive Memory*[1] by Jimmy Gear!

[2]

Audrey Baker is a police officer in the mountain hamlet of Griffith Falls, Washington. Several years have passed since her sister went missing and she is still trying to nurse the painful wounds that have come with the unsolved disappearance. The tragedy inspired her to join the local police department as she seeks some sort of closure by investing her life in protecting others.

Ryan Darrow is a modestly successful novelist from Chicago. He has come to Griffith Falls for both the scenery

---

1. https://books2read.com/u/bPlrPz

2. https://books2read.com/u/bPlrPz

and to gather research for his next book. He also has tragedy haunting him from the past as his wife had surrendered to cancer years before.

Audrey and Ryan find their paths crossing when Audrey fills in for the Chief, who is at a conference. In the midst of the normal routine of small-town police work, Audrey is called out to the home of Tonya Dorsey, whose brother-in-law died in a boating accident the night before.

What seems like an accident begins to grow more suspicious when a local child, Libby Henning, goes missing. Investigating the disappearance, Audrey can't help but feel that in some unexplainable way the two mysterious events are connected. When a local vagrant becomes a suspect in the investigation, it becomes apparent that not only are there little clues being left behind, but some of them seem intentional. Officer Baker must unravel the truth from the lies and find the little girl before it's too late.

About the Author

Jimmy Gear is a starving Master's student who started way too late to pursue his goal of being an English professor. He lives in Missouri.